力得文化
Leader Culture

Lead your way. Be your own leader!

力得文化
Leader Culture

Lead your way. Be your own leader!

力得文化
Leader Culture

科技業無往不利的英語力

每天只要 **20** 分鐘，**10** 週打造 **SMART** 好英語！

科技人非學不可、職場必備英語學習方案！

Teresa Chou ◎ 著

詳細彙整科技業「三用」英語句型
常用、實用、必用句型，在工作及生活上，輕鬆開口說，英文更 smart

超過70種的職場情境對話
將科技業「三用」英語句型置入職場情境，讓學習者能藉由熟悉的工作情境，
全方位掌握英語句型運用時機，讀一次就會，各類情境**不詞窮**

關鍵用語及字彙
讀完職場情境對話，再讀關鍵用語加字彙，與英語句型交互替換，
豐富語句生動性，簡報介紹**不呆板**

句型解析
不以文法做解析，而是詳細說明句型適用的時間及場合，
什麼狀況該用怎樣的說法，辦公交際**不搞砸**

句型延伸
一種句型，多種延伸說法，反覆練習便**熟能生巧**，
暢所欲言，表達零障礙

筆者依多年的
科技職場工作經驗
任高階管理職
最了解科技人英語上的需求
提供**最貼近科技職場**的
工作情境

另外還有 **10週** 完整規劃 X 每日 **20分鐘** 羽量學習 = **循序漸進的不 爆 肝學習**

　　繼上次「高劑量簡報英文」Part II and Part III 撰寫之後，感謝力得文化的邀約，繼續撰寫這本以科技人為主的每日英文用書。

　　在科技業多年的工作經驗，我有幸曾與不少優秀科技人共事，不少朋友曾分享他們對無法正確用英文表達自己意思的挫折感，雖然對科技專業用語沒太大問題，但當需要用英語對話正確表達，中間就有障礙存在，結果在外國同事前似乎就矮了一截。

　　因此讓我想撰寫這本書，根據科技人在工作上可能碰到的情境提供對話用語，使在工作崗位上表現不因英文表達而打折扣。當然英文能力的累積不是一蹴可幾，但重點是如何取得有效學習資訊，加以記憶、學習、運用。根據個人經驗，本書提供了 73 個情境，讀者能根據情境加以應用到其他自己的每日應對中。每天一句，都是非常實用的句子，加上常用字彙，相信對你會有所幫助。

Teresa Chou

編者序
EDITOR

　　隨著國內產業都趨於國際化的腳步，英文成了許多職場都相當重視的能力之一。尤其是在科技產業，因為其特殊的型態，英語力則成了不可或缺、甚至是必備的能力。

　　本書的作者曾任國內幾家科技大廠的高階主管職，也曾派駐在國外多年，深知在科技業中英語的重要性，對於國人在英語上常犯的錯誤及不熟悉的地方也有相當程度的了解。作者以輕鬆但不失專業的筆觸著作了這一本書，內容中除了包含在科技業實用的句型用法之外，還藏有作者豐富的工作智慧。

　　每一個單元都是以簡單的句型開始，慢慢加深，並且有簡單的進度規劃，每天只要 20 分鐘，只要 10 週便能打造出科技人必備的smart好英語！

力得文化編輯群

目　録

CONTENTS

目 錄
CONTENTS

On Behalf of...

謹代表……

 **Dialogue**

A: We are excited by the prospect of working with your company again.

B: The pleasure is ours. <u>On behalf of</u> the whole team, I would like to thank you for giving us a second chance to work with your company. We regret the hiccup we had during the last mock-up production due to a communication problem within our team.

A: We enjoy working with your team. Although it is a young group, it is very creative and enthusiastic. Most importantly, they are willing to go the extra mile. That's a welcome trait.

科技業無往不利的英語力

對話譯文

A: 我們為再次與貴公司合作的前景感到興奮。

B: 這是我們的榮幸,謹代表整個團隊,我要感謝你們願意再給我們一次機會。很抱歉上次在模型製作過程中,由於我們內部溝通有問題,造成些小插曲。

A: 我們的合作一直很愉快，雖然你們是個年輕團隊，但非常具有創意和熱情。最重要的是，他們就是願意多試這麼一些而不放棄，這是個很好的特質。

 科技關鍵知識用語

1. **prospect** n 前景，展望；可能的合作對象
There was no prospect of winning the election.
對於贏得選戰並不被看好。

2. **hiccup** n 打嗝；俗用說法是不小心的小意外
Sorry for the hiccup.
對突發意外感到抱歉。

3. **go the extra mile** 比需要的還多做一些
Because he went the extra mile, we are able to complete the task in time.
由於他的努力不懈，我們得以及時完成案子。

句型解析

On behalf of 代表某人或機構來說話、致詞或執行動作,屬於比較正式的用法。

另外,**speaking for** 和 **acting for** 用來分別表示代表某人發言和代表某人執行動作。

例如

Speaking for the organization, I would like to address the importance of building a low-carbon and eco-friendly environment.
我在此謹代表本組織來呼籲建立低碳和生態友好環境的重要性。

Acting for the project manager, I am going to re-define the product specification.
代理專案經理職務,我在此要重新定義產品規格。

 句型延伸及範例

1. I am calling in on behalf of Mr. Lewis. He is still in the other meeting which has lasted longer than expected.
   我代表 Mr. Lewis 打電話過來。由於另一會議開的比預期要久,所以他還在那會議中。

2. On behalf of Mr. Lewis, I will sign the agreement.
   我謹代表 Mr. Lewis 來簽署這份協議。

3. I am attending the discussion on behalf of Ms. Lee, who got stuck in traffic on her way here.

因為 Ms. Lee 在來的路上遇到塞車,所以我代表她來參與這個討論會。

4. On behalf of Ms. Lee, I would like to express our gratitude to the committee for your support.

我謹代表 Ms. Lee 向委員會表達我們的感激之情,感謝有你們的支持。

MEMO

What Am I Supposed to Do?

我該怎麼做呢？

 **Dialogue**

科技業無往不利的英語力

A: This is customer service. How may I assist you today?

B: Hi. I need help with the device I purchased from you.

A: Thanks for the call. May I know what problem you have experienced?

B: It might sound funny to you, but I have no idea how to get the device started. I have got it fully charged but I can't make a phone call.

A: I understand. First of all, have you completed the setup process?

B: What is that? What am I supposed to do?

A: Okay. We have included the User's Manual in each box. Just follow the step-by-step instructions in the User's Manual on page 5. This will guide you through the setup process.

B: Thank you so much. It sounds very simple.

A: It is a 3-step process. When it is done, you can start

enjoying the product. Thank you for calling.

 對話譯文

A：這裡是客服中心，有什麼我可以為您服務的嗎？

B：是的，我買了貴公司產品，在使用上需要您的協助。

A：謝謝您的來電，請問是什麼問題？

B：聽起來好像很好笑，我不知道如何啟用這產品。我把它充飽電，但還是不能用，我不知道如何用它來打電話。

A：別這麼說，首先請問您完成安裝程序嗎？

B：那是什麼？我該怎麼做呢？

A：好，每個產品包裝盒子中都有使用手冊，只要按照手冊上第五頁的步驟說明，就可完成您的安裝程序。

B：非常感謝，這聽起來很簡單。

A：只要 3 個步驟，您就可以開始使用這產品了。感謝您的來電。

1. **instruction** n 指示，說明

2. **User's Manual** 使用者手冊

   另外通常也會附上一份簡易版的使用指南，**QSG (Quick Start Guide)**

3. **guide you through** 指引你

   這可以是一本說明書指引你如何操作，也可用於一個人指引你的一些問題，亦或是宗教上神的指引生命的探尋。

 句型解析

Suppose 一字為假設意思。**What am I supposed to do?**（我該怎麼做呢？）而當除去 what 則有不同意思，

例如

    Am I supposed to do everything?

    我應該做所有的事嗎？

當說話者用比較溫和語氣時，代表說話者以詢問語氣詢問是否該做所有的事；若說話者用較強硬尖銳的語氣，則意謂說話者不認為他該做所有的事。

 句型延伸及範例

Suppose 還有許多其它常用的方式，在被動語態中，除了上述的用法，

還有當表示事件不如預期般發生。

例如

After putting in the command, it is supposed to respond as I described. But I have no idea what's going on now.

輸入這指令後，它的反應應該跟我所說的一樣，現在我不知道是怎麼回事。

The deposit was supposed to be made.

照理說訂金應該已經付了。

也可以作為連接詞，以帶出一個假設條件句。

例如

Suppose Stacy can't borrow her mother's car, how will we go to that shopping mall?

如果 Stacy 不能借用她媽媽的車的話，那我們要怎麼去購物中心呢？

MEMO

Speaking of Which...

 Dialogue

科
技
業
無
往
不
利
的
英
語
力

A: Wow... the demonstration looks fantastic! The motion is smooth and the depth of image is just right.

B: Yes, the game looks great in virtual 3-D. It should attract plenty of attention in the exhibition next week. Speaking of which, do you know what to expect at that show from our competitor?

A: To be honest, I am not much worried about the competition. I hear from a reliable source that they don't have anything to wow anybody. They apparently have some personnel issues to settle in the R&D team. The leader left a couple of months ago and took some talented people with him. They need more expertise now in virtualized IT environments. We're in the lead right now.

 對話譯文

A：哇……這 demo 看起來棒極了，動作很順，影像深度也恰到好處。

B： 是的，這遊戲的 **3D** 虛擬實境看起來很棒。我相信在下週展覽會上我們會吸引很多的關注。說到展覽，你知道我們的競爭對手將在展覽會推出什麼遊戲嗎？

A： 說實話，我不太擔心。一個可靠的消息來源說，他們今年沒什麼讓你驚訝的東西。他們的研發頭帶了幾個能手兩個月前離開之後，研發團隊似乎有內部人事問題，我認為他們需要更多有虛擬科技環境專業知識的人。我們現在領先他們。

科技關鍵知識用語

1. demonstration **n** 示範；實物說明；示威（運動），示威遊行

在職場上常用 demo 來同時表示「示範」的動詞和名詞，

例如

I would like to demo how this machine works.
This will conclude today's demo.

而完整說法應是

I would like to demonstrate how this machine works.
我要示範一下這個機器的使用方法。

This will conclude the demonstration of today.

這裡總結今天的示範。

2. expertise n 專業知識

在職場上是很好用的字，

例如

It is my expertise.

這是我的專業。

Our expertise is to customize the software based on customer's request.

我們的專業是根據客戶要求來客製化軟體

3. in the lead 領先

另外也可以說 take the lead

例如

We are in the lead. / We are taking the lead.

我們居於領先地位。

 句型解析

Speaking of which 指的是剛剛所談到的主題，是外國人在對話時很常用且很好用的表達方式，讓句子較有變化性。本對話中的 which 代表 exhibition，句子中也可換為 speaking of exhibition…。

對於英文為第二語言的人常用的是 by the way，但之後所述內容與前面

科技業無往不利的英語力

主題不需要有關連，只是一種轉折語氣。而 **speaking of which** 可讓你的對話聽起來更smart.

另外常聽到的還有 **speak of the devil**，意思是正談著某人時，且不預期地他就出現了。有中文裡類似「說曹操，曹操就到」的意思。

例如

Speak of the devil and he appears.

 句型延伸及範例

1. The picture quality sucks in this model that we are building. Speaking of which, who is your supplier for the lens module? Your device seems to perform much better.

   我們負責的產品影像品質很糟；說到這個，你的鏡頭元件供應商是誰啊？你的產品的影像表現好像比我們的好很多？

2. Our boss is at the press conference. Speaking of her, I heard she will be promoted.

   我們的老闆正在參加記者發表會；說到老闆，我聽說她會被升官。

3. A: What is your opinion about the new boss?

   B: Well, it's hard to say much yet, but he seems to be a slow decision maker.

   A: Speak of the devil...

   A：你的新上司如何？

   B：嗯，這還很難說，但他做決策很慢。

   A：說曹操，曹操就到。

As Opposed to...

是……而不是……

 **Dialogue**

A: We regret to inform you that, due to limited manufacturing capacity, we are not able to deliver the orders on hand by end of the month.

B: We will likely fail to launch the product this month and this will affect our profit earnings this quarter. Are there any remedies we can consider?

A: I am afraid not. Our only solution is to increase production facility, but the lead time for equipment and staff preparation is two months.

B: Unfortunately, missing the goal will put us in violation of the contract. I suggest we make a contingency plan. Perhaps we should outsource the difference to an independent manufacturer **as opposed to** waiting for a new facility.

A: Sure. That's doable.

B: I am glad we are able to agree and achieve a meeting of minds.

As Opposed to...

 對話譯文

A：很遺憾地告訴你，由於產能的不足，我們無法完成手上預定在月底出貨的訂單。

B：我們很可能無法如期在這個月上市新產品，這也會對本季的獲利影響很大。有其他辦法可考慮嗎？

A：恐怕沒有。唯一的解決辦法是增加生產線，但需要至少需要2個月的時間來準備設備和人工。

B：很不幸的，無法出貨將違反了我們所簽訂的合約。我建議採取緊急計劃，或許我們可將差額外包給其他廠家而不是苦等新的產線。

A：嗯，這是可行的。

B：我很高興我們達成共識。

 科技關鍵知識用語

1.orders on hand　手上已收到的訂單
在科技業常聽到訂單能見度就是由手上收到的訂單來看。

科技業無往不利的英語力

2.**remedy** Ⓝ 補救，糾正

Hiring more people isn't always the best remedy for reducing employees' workload.The problem was beyond remedy.

錄用更多的人不是減少員工的工作量的最好辦法，問題不僅僅是這樣而已。

3.**violate** Ⓥ 觸犯，違反

Your behavior has violated the law.

你的行為已觸法。

4.**contingency plan** 緊急應變計劃

在快速變化的科技業，緊急應變計畫的需求是時常可見，"seek for a contingency plan" 絕對是很好用的説法。

5.**a meeting of minds** 達成共識

We have achieved a meeting of minds and everybody is happy.

我們已達成共識，皆大歡喜。

💡 句型解析

As opposed to 是……而不是……

有較強烈及正式的説法，通常前後兩者之間有相對的關係，或有顯著的相異性，不僅僅是喜好選擇。

例如

He supports New Party as opposed to KMT.

他支持新黨而不是國民黨。

當然使用 rather than 也沒有太大問題，但在氣勢上就弱了些。另外 rather than 和 instead of，雖然也是「是……，而不是……」，但比較是兩者間的喜好選擇。

例如

Take the bus instead of the train./ Take the bus rather than the train.

搭公車而不是火車。

I like to eat vegetables instead of eating meat - I like to eat vegetables, rather than eating meat.

我喜歡吃蔬菜，不喜歡吃肉

 句型延伸及範例

1. For our situation, to improve employees' satisfaction with their jobs is to invest more in training and education to help them performing better as opposed to reduce their job responsibilities.

   對於我們的情況，提高員工對工作的滿意度是投資更多培訓和教育，以幫助他們在工作上的表現，而不是減少他們的工作職責。

2. When your subordinates resign, you should look into the real reasons behind as opposed to blame on their lacking loyalty for the company.

   當你的下屬辭職，你應該看看背後的真正原因，而不是指責他們對公司缺乏忠誠度。

I'm Not in
A Position to…

我沒辦法（沒有這樣的職權）…

Dialogue

A: It's my pleasure to introduce you the most recent product we have come out in this quarter. The enhancement of the product is to offer users a variety of user interfaces. Depending on the preference, the users are able to set as default.

B: Would you please elaborate more?

A: If you are a heavy user on communication features, the device will automatically group the applications including dialer, messaging and chatting apps, social network apps or anything related to communication on your main screen. On the other hand, if you are a heavy multimedia user, you will find the related multimedia applications available at your fingertips.

B: Now it sounds interesting. One question for you: do you have one scenario selection that customizes the experience for seniors—say, giving them larger fonts, louder speakers, health- and medical-related applications grouped together as defaults, et cetera?

科技業 無往不利的英語力

A: I do see where you are coming from. As a matter of fact, that would change the whole architecture. I am afraid **I am not in a position to** answer your question, but I will pass on your request to the project leader.

對話譯文

A： 我很高興向您介紹本季最新的產品，這產品主要是針對使用者介面加以強化，使用者可依個人偏好作為預設介面選擇。

B： 可以詳細說明嗎？

A： 如果你是個重度電話或聊天用戶，系統會自動將相關應用軟體做為群組，設置於螢幕表面，例如撥號器、簡訊和有聊天功能軟體、社群軟體和其他相關通信軟體。如果你是個重度多媒體用戶，相關的多媒體應用程式會讓你隨手可得。

B： 現在聽起來很有趣。但有個問題：是否有專為年長人使用的介面，譬如較大的字體、較高音量的揚聲器，且以保健和醫療相關的應用程式群組為預設介面等等之類的？

A：我很了解您為何有此需求。但事實上，它可能會改變整個架構，這恐怕我不是我能回答你的問題。不過，我會把你的要求傳達給專案負責人。

 科技關鍵知識用語

1. elaborate Ⅴ 闡明，説明

If you like to know more about the product, we will elaborate more with some examples in the next session.

如果您想對這產品有更多了解，在接下來的部分，我們採用一些例子來闡述。

2. at your fingertips 隨手可得，近在手邊，隨時可供使用

He is hooked on Facebook and he has it at his fingertips.

他迷上了Facebook，他把臉書不離手。

3. etc./et cetera adv 等等

etc. 是 et cetera（發音則是 [ɛt ˈsɛt ɚ ə]）的縮寫，在英文書寫時通常只用縮寫 etc.，而對英文為第二語言的人來説，常常會忽略如何發音，因此在口語對話上會用 and so forth 和 and so on 來代替。但當國外客戶説到 et cetera，你也要知道對方説的是什麼。

句型解析

I am not in a position to···

這說法是用來闡明自己並非可以回答這問題或完成這任務的人，而是必須請示有此決策權的高層或主管。而或是你並不具備有這些知識，亦或是任何原因無法如此做。丟掉你過去常説的"I don't know and I have to ask..."改用"I am not in a position to···"這會讓你的對話更正式，聽起來也更專業。

 句型延伸及範例

1. I am not in a position to show you around our research center because it is only for authorized personnel.

   我沒辦法帶你參觀我們的研究中心，因為它需要授權才能進去。

2. I am not in a position to tell you what to do; you might have to make your own decision.

   我無法告訴你該怎麼做，你必須做出自己的決定。

3. I am not in a position to sign off the approval.

   我不是可以簽字批准的人。

If
/Whether or Not

如果……/……是否

Dialogue

A: Hey, I haven't seen you for a while? What have you been busy doing?

B: Er, I am in the office every day, almost 18 hours a day! The product my team has been assigned is way behind the development schedule. This morning, we have been informed that the customer has requested to move forward the product launch schedule. The worst thing is that the leader has made a commitment to the customer without confirming with the team.

A: This afternoon in the product development review meeting, someone brought up the over-promised schedule. As I understand it, people are still discussing **whether or not** to keep the original schedule.

B: That would be great **if** there's some space for negotiation.

 對話譯文

A：嘿，有好一陣子沒看到你了，最近在忙些什麼？

B：呃，我每天都在辦公室啊！幾乎每天有 **18** 個小時在這裡！我的團隊負責開發的產品進度落後很多，今天上午開會我們才被告知，客戶要求產品提前上市。更糟糕的是沒有和我們做進一步的確認，產品負責人就承諾客戶的要求提早完成產品開發。

A：在今天下午的產品開發討論會上，有人提出這過度承諾的問題，據我的理解，仍在討論是否要保留原來的時間表。

B：如果仍有商量餘地就太好了。

 科技關鍵知識用語

1. launch **v** 開始；發射

是科技業常用字，尤其是業務行銷相關工作。**Launch the product** 意指產品上市。此外，**launch** 也用於發射飛彈、魚雷，船舶下水，例如 **launch the missile**、**launch the boat**。

另外還有 **launcher**（發射器或驅動軟體），這也是在科技業職場中常會使用到的字，

科技業無往不利的英語力

例如

We can also write a launcher to activate the program.

我們可另外再寫個啟動軟體來驅動這程式。

2. move forward　提前，將時間表提前

Looks like the situation has left us without an option other than to move forward the product launch to put us one month ahead of the competitor.

照這情況看來，我們沒有任何選擇，必須把產品發表提前，比競爭者早一個月。

3. push back　延後

Let's push back the date for going abroad.

讓我們延後出國日期。

 句型解析

whether 作為「是否」的意思，常常與 if 用法類似；而當 whether 接著 or not「不論」，則與 if 有不同解釋。

簡單的區分法，若在說明某種情況時，用"if"，其他情況則使用 whether。

以下兩句中，兩者用法相同，意味著是否。

1. I would like to know if you like the idea.

我想知道你是否喜歡這點子。

2. I would to know whether or not you like this idea.

我想知道你喜不喜歡這點子。

而下面句子兩者則有顯著差別，

1. If it rains tomorrow, we won't attempt the field test.

   如果明天下雨，我們則不做實測。

～此時的 if 作為「如果」使用。「如果明天下雨」是情況的介紹。

2. Whether or not it rains tomorrow, we will attempt the field test.

   不管明天下不下雨，實測照舊。

～whether… or not 解釋為「不論……是否」，是種確定說明而不是情況的介紹。

 句型延伸及範例

1. We like to know whether we will have meeting with CEO so I can be prepared.

   我們想知道我們是否會與CEO開會，所以我好做準備。

2. It doesn't matter whether we go or not.

   我們去還是不去都不要緊。

3. You have to work overtime to finish the job, whether you like it or not.

   你必須加班完成工作，不管你喜不喜歡。

Speaking in Terms of...

說到⋯⋯

Dialogue

科技業無往不利的英語力

A: What do you think about the factory visit?

B: It is a very organized management, no doubt. It's obvious that their ambition is to be the biggest manufacture in this field, given the investment they have made in their new facility.

A: Indeed. But I have paid attention to how many stations they went through to complete the process, and that has made me think about the efficiency of their administration. Apart from that, though, I am very impressed with what I have seen.

B: I share the same thought. **Speaking in terms of** the efficiency of their production process, it's rather obvious they have lot of improvement to make.

 對話譯文

A： 你對這家工廠有什麼看法？

B： 毫無疑問這是一個非常有組織的管理，而且很明顯地他們做了很大的投資在新的設備，非常積極想成為這個領域最大的製造商。

A： 的確。但是，我特別注意到他們產線上完成一道程序的站點很多，這讓我必須要思考一下有關他們的效率問題。除此之外，我對所看到的有很好的印象。

B： 我也有同感，說到生產效率，他們有相當大的改進空間。

 科技關鍵知識用語

1. make me think about 讓我思索

His speech today makes me think about how he got to become who he is today.

他今天的演講讓我不禁思考，他是怎麼成為今天的他。

2. apart from that/what 除此之外

Apart from that, our design has no problem at all.

33

除此之外，我們的設計一點問題都沒有。

3.be impressed with　感到印象深刻

We are very impressed by what Steve has presented in the press conference. His idea has brought technology into another level.

我們對於 Steve 在新聞發表會上的介紹有非常深刻的印象。他的想法將科技帶入了另一層次。

科技業無往不利的英語力

 句型解析

對話中的句子也可寫為：" If we look at how efficient the production process is, it's rather obvious they have lot of improvement to make." 。而以 **speaking in terms of** 這樣的說法，在對話中聽起來，比上句要來得簡潔俐落，也能很清楚地傳達出你知道自己在說什麼。

Speaking in terms of（說到關於……）與 with regard to（關於……）有類似的用法。

句型延伸及範例

1. Speaking in terms of the company culture, we have recognized the changes since the new CEO got on board.

談到公司文化，自從新的執行長上任之後，我們充分地感受到這樣的改變。

2. With regard to the recent airplane crashes, it has increased much more people's attention on aviation safety.

關於最近飛機墜毀了，這讓人們對航空安全有更大的重視。

MEMO

Do You Mind...

你介意……嗎？

Dialogue

A: Hi, Tom. I am calling you to inform you that we are unable to supply you the last batch of components as initially scheduled.

B: Does it mean you need longer lead time to deliver? Or do you have replacement instead?

A: As a matter of fact, it is nothing about the lead time and we have no replacement to supply.

B: **Do you mind** to go straight to the matter? What on earth is the problem at your end?

A: You might have heard one of the chipsets is in shortage; as a result, its price has gone up double. By all means, we have tried to get our hands on it but without luck. At the moment, we have no visibility for the availability.

 對話譯文

A：嗨，Tom。我打電話來是為了告訴你，我們無法依原訂時間交出最後一批元件。

B：你是說你們需要更長的交貨時間嗎？或者你要用其他替換的元件來交貨呢？

A：其實我們目前沒有交貨時間，也有沒有替代元件供應。

B：你介意直接切入問題嗎？究竟你那邊發生什麼問題？

A：你可能也聽說其中一種晶片大缺貨，因此它的價格已經上漲了一倍。透過各種方法，我們試圖希望能拿到一些貨，但還是沒有。目前，我們沒有任何供貨能見度。

 科技關鍵知識用語

1. **go straight to the matter** 直接切入問題

在出現狀況時，我們會看到有些人不知如何啟齒，會繞著問題轉，此時則可說 "go straight to the matter!"。

在另一種情況當有人說話時，但卻無法表達重點則可說 "please go straight to the points."（請直接切入重點。）

2. **what on earth…**　到底是什麼

What on earth are you talking about?

你到底在說些什麼啊？

3. **by all means**　透過所有方式；只管；務必

Do it, by all means, but don't let the cat out of the bag.

只管做下去，但千萬不要洩漏秘密。

4. **visibility**　能見度

可有幾種不同情況用法：

· **order visibility** 訂單能見度

· **delivery visibility** 出貨能見度

· **revenue visibility** 營收能見度

科技業無往不利的英語力

句型解析

Do you mind...?（你介意……嗎？）後面接動名詞，表示詢問的語氣「是否可以……？」。

另外 **do you mind** 後面還可加 **if sb.** ＋ 動詞

例如

Do you mind if I sit here?

你介意我坐這裡嗎？

你的回答可以是簡單的"No, I don't."（不，我不介意），然而更活潑口語化的回答則是"Sure, please go ahead."（當然，請坐）。

而當你若不希望他坐這裡時，通常會也禮貌上地舉出理由，而非只是拒絕的回答。

例如

Sorry, the seat is taken.

不好意思，這有人坐。

Sorry, my friend is sitting here.

不好意思，我朋友坐這裡。

另外與 "do you mind...?" 相關的問句

例如

Do you mind my asking what the cost was?

你介意我問成本是多少嗎？

這裡用"my"，因為後面接的"asking"，強調在「我的問題」。

也有人説"Do you mind me asking what the cost was?"強調在「我」的問題。

基本上兩者些微的差別在於強調的重點。

 句型延伸及範例

1. Do you mind to come to my office?

你介意到我的辦公室一下嗎？

2. Do you mind staying a few days in the factory?

你介意待在工廠幾天嗎？

3. Do you mind if we postpone the meeting to next week?

你介意將會議延後至下星期嗎？

Given the Importance of...

有鑑於⋯⋯的重要性

 **Dialogue**

A: The exhibition is right around the corner and I still have a long list of jobs to do. I need to be in so many places at the same time! I deserve a vacation after this.

B: Yes, running a stand in a trade show is a demanding work. Your job makes the company in the eyes of the whole world. Last year, due to our management problems, we fell out of the top three in the worldwide market.
Given the importance of returning to that league, the exhibition is the perfect event for us. It showcases our product line-up with all its innovation. We all have our fingers crossed.

A: Speaking of which, I have to run. It just came to mind that I have some more details to attend to.

 對話譯文

A：這次展覽即將到來，一長串的工作清單要我處理，我根本是分身乏術。展覽後我應該度個假。

B：是啊，辦展是一個繁忙的工作，你的工作得以讓公司在全世界面前展現。去年由於管理問題，我們掉到全球市場的前三名之外。
有鑑於重返寶座的重要性，展覽是一個最好的方式用以展示我們最創新的產品陣容，我們大家都很期待能順利成功。

A：說到這個，我要走了。突然想到有好多細節要處理。

 科技關鍵知識用語

1.right around the corner 即將到來；就在眼前

Chinese New Year is right around the corner. The streets are full of holiday decorations.

中國新年即將到來。街上都充滿著新年的裝飾。

科技業無往不利的英語力

2. be in so many places at the same time　分身乏術

I need to be in so many places at the same time this week, so I must delegate tasks to other members of the team as best I can.

我這一個星期分身乏術，我必須將工作儘量分配給其他的組員。

3. showcase　ⓝ　展示

The Art Exhibition is the showcase for those young artists.

藝術展是讓年輕藝術家可以展現才華的好機會。

4. product line-up　產品陣容

The company refreshed nearly its entire product line-up in the last few months.

這家公司在過去幾個月當中幾乎更新了全部的產品陣容。

5. keep one's fingers crossed　祝我們好運

We are going to present our new product concept to customers. Keep your fingers crossed!

我們要去向客戶展示我們的新產品了。祝我們好運吧！

6. come to my mind　浮現腦海，想到

Thousands of confused thoughts come to my mind.

千頭萬緒湧上我的心頭。

句型解析

"**Given the importance of...**"這樣的說法直接了當的強調接下來主題的重要性，當然這對話也可用簡單的"It is important for the company to return to the league..."，但當聽者聽到Given the importance of...時，自然的會豎起耳朵來傾聽，而這種說法也增加語句變化性，不是老是用"It is..."來開始一個句子。

 句型延伸及範例

1. Given the importance of education for a country to flourish, how should we fund education?

   有鑑於教育對於國家繁盛的重要性，我們該怎樣去資助教育呢？

2. Given the importance of nurturing children in a safe environment, should we support the death penalty?

   有鑑於在安全無虞的環境下養育孩子的重要性，我們是否應該支持死刑呢？

Due to Unforeseen Circumstances, ...

由於不可預知的情況……

Dialogue

Project Manager: Jen, may I speak to you?

Jen: Sure.

Project Manager: Sorry to barge in without an appointment. We have a critical problem and need your decision.

Jen: Fill me in.

Project Manager: We might have to cancel the project.

Jen: That's not an option we can afford. What's the problem?

Project Manager: I understand how much cancellation would impact our financial status, but we may have no other option. **Due to unforeseen circumstances**, a key component supplier has discontinued its product line. This is our sole supplier for the component. We can't buy the same thing from someone else. Going to any other supplier means changing the product specs, and that affects the architecture. Essentially, we would be starting a

new project.

Jen: Well, if you're sure there's no other way to acquire this component, we will have to start all over. Please re-use as much of the present design as you can to keep costs down. Speaking of which, we need a review of all our projects on hand to see how they are affected by this supply situation. Can you please prepare for that?

Project: Sure, will do.
Manager

 對話譯文

專案經理：老闆，我可以和你談一下嗎？

Jen ：當然。
（主管）

專案經理：對不起，沒事先預約，只是我們有個很棘手的問題需要您來決定。

Jen：告訴我什麼事。

專案經理：我們可能不得不取消手上的案子。

Jen：我們無法承受這樣的做法，是什麼問題？

專案經理：我了解取消對公司財務狀況的影響很大，但沒其他選擇，由於不可預知的情況，我們其中一個主要元件供應商已停止生產我們用的元件。不幸的是，這家公司是我們的唯一供應商，我們沒有其他的選擇。如果我們要找其他的供應商，很可能我們必須改變所有規格，影響結構。基本上這等於是啟動新的案子。

Jen：如果你確定我們沒有其他選擇，只好重新開始，但要盡量使用原有設計來降低成本。說到這個，我想審核一下手上所有案子受影響情況。能否請你準備？

專案經理：當然。

 科技關鍵知識用語

1. barge in 闖入、不請自來

Oh! I'm sorry. I didn't mean to barge in on you.

哦！對不起，我不是故意要闖進來。

Please don't interrupt me! You can't just barge in like that!

請你不能就這麼闖進來打斷我！

2. fill me in 告訴我事情原委

Fill me in on what has just happened in the meeting.

告訴我剛剛在會議中發生什麼事。

Fill me in about John's argument with Jason.

告訴我 John 為什麼和 Jason 起了爭執。

3.**start all over** 全新開始

After the rain, it's very likely we have to start the sand sculpture all over again.

雨後，我們的沙雕很可能得從新再做。

 句型解析

"Due to unforeseen circumstance, ..." 是很正式的説法用來解釋所發生的事在預料之外。但可能也要很小心使用這方式來解釋工作上發生的問題，畢竟老闆想知道的是問題發生你能有解決方案，除非是天災人禍，做計畫時能有備案在腹，而不是讓自己卡在死角中無法動彈。

 句型延伸及範例

1.The concert has been cancelled due to unforeseen circumstances; we'll reveal more details in the next news update.

由於不可預見的情況演唱會已被取消，我們將在下一段的新聞中報導更詳細的資訊。

2.Due to unforeseen circumstances, the stock market dropped 100 points in one day.

由於不可預見的狀況，股市在一天內下跌了 100 點。

Given the Circumstances...

在這情況下……

 **Dialogue**

科技業無往不利的英語力

Mary: Hi, George. I am stopping by to pick up the sample for my visit to customers in Europe. I head out next week.

George: Here is the sample. Let me demonstrate.

Mary: It still seems pretty rough.

George: I am afraid so. We were short-handed with engineers. This was the best we could do given the circumstances. If you really want to show it, please explain to the customer that this is a test prototype. Given another month of fine-tuning and de-bugging, we can have the device behaving more like a finished product.

Mary: I was looking forward to showing this, but as things stand now I prefer to wait. I don't want this customer to lose confidence in us.

George: I understand. We tried, but if the gadget isn't ready for prime time, so be it.

 對話譯文

Mary： 嗨，George。我特地來拿下星期去歐洲出差要帶給客人看的樣品。

George： 這是樣品，讓我示範一下。

Mary： 看起來還很糟糕。

George： 沒辦法，由於最近工程師人手不足，在這情況下我們已盡最大努力了。如果你真的要示範給客戶，可以解釋這只是個樣機，再一個月的時間來調整和解決問題，則可看到如成品般的樣品。

Mary： 我本來很期待示範給客人看，但就這情況下，我寧願等一下，以免客戶對我們的信心打折扣。

George： 我了解，我們已盡最大努力，現在還不適合亮相，就只能這樣了。

 科技關鍵知識用語

1. head out for / head for　前往/出發
She is heading out for Paris.
她即將前往巴黎。

科技業無往不利的英語力

2. **rough** adj 粗糙、粗魯、簡陋

This is just a rough sketch. I will make a finished painting later.

這只是一個粗略的草圖，等一下我會把它畫完成。

3. **short-handed** 缺人手，人手不足

We are very short-handed and would like you to join us.

我們很缺人手，希望你能加入我們的行列。

4. **fine-tuning** 微調

After the fine-tuning, the TV has regained its picture quality.

微調後，電視畫面恢復了品質。

5. **de-bugging** 糾正問題

We have spent the whole night to de-bug the device and finally there is some progress.

我們已經花了整個晚上改正產品上的錯誤，終於有一些進展了。

6. **lose confidence** 失去信心

I lost confidence in his ability to manage the crisis after he gave that speech.

在他說了那番話之後，我對他危機處理能力失去了信心。

7. **prime time** 黃金時段（not ready for prime time：表示還不夠好）

I enjoy this comedy club, even if some of the acts aren't yet ready for prime time.

我喜歡這個喜劇俱樂部的表演，即使一些節目還上不了臺面。

I enjoyed your presentation. Want to give it again at the

regional meeting? Are you ready for prime time?

我很喜歡妳的簡報。想在區域會議中做簡報，準備好大放異彩了嗎？

8.**so be it** 就只能這樣（你不接受也沒辦法）

I'm only giving you the numbers. If you don't like them, so be it.

我只能給你數字，你不喜歡也沒辦法。

 句型解析

當用 __given the circumstances__（以這情況來說）時，表示不是在理想的情況下，所以結果需要一些妥協，或在做決定或比較時可能需要降低標準來看。另外，**under the circumstances** 是相同用法。

 句型延伸及範例

1.You are not able to fit into the dress. Given the circumstances, you will need to wear another dress to the party.

你穿不下這禮服。在這情況下，你會需要穿別件禮服去宴會了。

2.The sky looks overcast. Given the circumstances, we should try to finish this outdoor luncheon within one hour.

天空看起來陰沉沉的。在這情況下，我們應該盡量在一小時內完成這個戶外午餐。

51

Such Is the Complexity of the Issue That...

這就是形勢的複雜性……

Dialogue

A: Hi, team. I am here to update you about the situation we face in the Russian market. We have positioned ourselves as a long-term player in this market. As such, sustaining market share is a priority for us. The recent drop in oil prices has had a major impact on the Russian economy. In addition, last week a price war started between two of our competitors. Our sales have been affected greatly by both developments. We will have to come down on the street price in order to move our stock.

B: What is our strategy to deal with the situation?

A: **Such is the complexity of the issue that** we have to re-examine everything, from overall economic situation to product availability, pricing policy, channel promotion and stock availability.

科技業無往不利的英語力

 對話譯文

A：大家好，我在這裡針對我們在俄羅斯市場正面臨的情況做報告，我們希望在這市場永續經營，為此，保持我們的市場佔有率是首要任務。由於最近的油價下跌，已經大大影響俄羅斯的經濟。而上週我們的兩個競爭對手開始在市場上展開價格戰，這兩件事對我們的銷售產生極大的影響。為了能持續銷售，我們可能不得不降低零售價。

B：我們該用什麼策略來應付這情況呢？

A：這就是形勢的複雜性，我們可能必須從整體經濟情況，到產品銷售、價格策略、渠道推廣和庫存的情況整體考量。

 科技關鍵知識用語

1. impact n v 影響

The impact of the war in the Gulf is too hard to evaluate.
海灣戰爭的影響太大難以評估。

The increase of taxi fare affected greatly on the decision for people to take taxi as daily transportation.
計程車資的增加會大幅影響到人們將計程車作為日常交通工具的決定。

★ impact 和 **affect** 的用法相同，大致上都可互相取代。

2. **price war**　價格戰

The price war has given no benefit to any parties in the market.

價格戰對市場上的任何商家都沒好處。

3. **as such**　為此

Jessie Lu is a single parent and she is the only person her little daughter can rely on. As such, she cannot afford to gamble with her health.

Jessie Lu是個單親媽媽，她是她幼小女兒唯一的依靠。為此，她不能拿她的健康來賭。

4. **deal with**　應付，處理

He started to panic when dealing with his parent's illness.

當要處理他的親人病情時，他開始慌了。

 句型解析

"**Such is the complexity of the situation that…**"：就這情況的複雜性而言……

"**Such is the difficulty of the issue that…**"：就這問題的困難度而言……

Such 代表之前描述的問題或情況，這說法後的語句是根據這情況或問題所提出的解決方案或看法。

另外常用的方式為 given the situation…，但說法則較顯平淡簡單。不論在書信或口語對話上 such is the…, that…都可增加英文的變化性，聽起來更專業。

 句型延伸及範例

1. Such is the complexity of the issue that I can't think of any strategy to solve the problem.

   就這問題的複雜性，我想不出任何策略來解決這個問題。

2. Such is the difficulty of the issue that we will need to provide more incentives in order to lift morale.

   就這問題的困難度，我們必須提供更多的獎勵來提高士氣。

3. Such is the nature of human beings, we will probably never completely eliminate procrastination in the workplace.

   就這是人性的本質，我們無法杜絕在工作場所中拖延的習慣。

If You Don't Mind...

如果你不介意的話……

 **Dialogue**

科技業無往不利的英語力

A: The reason I've called this meeting is to confirm with you the conditions written into the proposal. The customer will make a proposal based on these conditions to enter the government bidding tender. If for any reason we are unable to follow through on our commitment, penalties will apply according to the agreement we signed. Please have a careful look at your area of responsibility and raise any concerns if you have them.

B: Thanks for giving us another look at this. In the production meeting this morning we learned about a labor shortage we face in the assembly line. **If you don't mind**, we would like to have one more day to confirm the new production schedule. Any labor issues could affect the delivery time in your proposal. We don't want to make commitments we can't fulfill.

 對話譯文

A： 今天我請大家參加這會議的原因是想與大家確認這企劃書中所述的條件，我們的客戶會根據我們提出的企劃書來進行政府招標投標書。若我們無法兌現我們的承諾，根據合約會有罰款產生。所以請各位仔細看看你們所負責的部分，若有任何問題，請提出來。

B： 謝謝你讓我們有機會再確認，因為今天早上的生產計劃會議我們討論到目前正面臨的生產線勞工短缺的情況。如果你不介意的話，我們需要再多一天的時間來確認新的生產排程，勞工短缺可能影響企劃書中的交貨時間，我們不希望過度承諾。

 科技關鍵知識用語

1.follow through　貫徹（從頭到尾完成任務）

She has clever advertising ideas, but we will need a larger design staff in order to follow through with some of them.

她的廣告創意很新穎，但我們會需要更多的設計團隊人員來完成。

2.your area of responsibility　你負責的部分

Have you read through your responsible area? Any typo?

W
E
E
K
2

If You Don't Mind...

57

你有讀完你負責的部分嗎？有任何錯字嗎？

3. raise　Ⅴ　提出，升起

Should you have any different opinion, please raise your hand.

如果有任何不同的看法，請舉手。

4. affect　Ⅴ　影響

The outcome of the election will affect greatly to the country's next ten years of development.

選舉的結果將大大地影響到這國家未來十年的發展。

★ affect 為動詞／effect 名詞

How will this weapon affect the tigers? / What is this weapon's effect on the tigers?

這種武器對老虎有何影響？

5. fulfill　Ⅴ　履行，完成，滿足

He won't be able to fulfill his ambition to climb up to Mount Everest.

他將無法達成他爬上聖母峰的野心。

 句型解析

If you don't mind… 雖然句子本身不是疑問句，但其實是個客氣的詢問語氣來詢問對方是否介意後面接想做的動作，相似於前面談過的 **"do you mind if…?"**

但兩者之間還是有些微差別，**if you don't mind** 帶有必要如此做的意味，可能是因為其實沒有其他選擇，例如在一個會議簡報場合，你可能需要一張椅子置放簡報所需東西，此時你會說: **If you don't mind, I would need this chair.**

而"**do you mind if**"則似乎是給對方決定**yes or no** 的權利，例如：**"Do you mind if I smoke here?"**對方的回答則可能是一半一半。

 ## 句型延伸及範例

1. If you don't mind, I would like to take a different approach.
   如果你不介意，我想用不同方式進行。

2. Do you mind if I take different approaches?
   你介意我用不同方式進行嗎？

3. If you don't mind, I would like to be excused.
   如果你不介意，我想退席了。

4. Do you mind if I am excused?
   你介意我退席嗎？

You Can Rest Assured That...

你可以放心……

 **Dialogue**

A: Last time the technician arrived ten minutes past 12 noon, and I had already left. Can you make sure he will not be late this time?

B: I'm sorry to hear you had to spend another weekend without a telephone connection. This time I will specifically instruct the technician that you cannot stay past noon. **You can rest assured that** he will be on time. You have my word.

A: Thank you. I am sorry to tell you I will have to file a complaint if there are any more screw-ups.

對話譯文

A： 上次你們的技術人員中午 12 點十分才到，而我當時已經離開了。你可以確保他這次不會遲到了嗎？

B： 我很抱歉聽到你有一個週末沒有電話可用；這次我會特地指示技術人員 12 點後你不在，你可以放心他會準時到，我保證。

A： 謝謝你，不過我得先說，如果再搞砸，我會提起客訴的。

科技關鍵知識用語

1. **sure** `adj` `adv`　確實的；這裡列舉出三個包含 sure 的片語

★ make sure　確保
Please make sure you have made an appointment with him.
請確保你已經跟他預約了。

★ sure enough　絕對的，非常確定的
Sure enough, the party is cancelled.
非常確定聚會已經取消了。

★ for sure　確定，不容置疑
He is going to do well, for sure.
不容置疑他會做得很好。

2. **specifically** `adv`　特地的
I have specifically reminded him to follow the rules.
我已經特地提醒他遵守規則。

3. **You have my words.**　我保證
相同於我們說的「一諾千金」，在早期歐洲貴族說的話也就是他們的承諾，代表這人的誠信，就如同書面承諾般。

科技業無往不利的英語力

No harm will come to your demo model. You have my words.

我保證絕對不會弄壞你的樣機的。

也可用"take my word for it"

Do you have evidence to back up what you say, or must we take your word for it?

你有證據證實你所說的嗎？還是我們就必須相信你所說？

4. **file a complaint**　　提出客訴；提出控訴

I am going to file a complaint with the Consumer Protection Committee.

我將向消費者保護會提出申訴。

5. **screw up** Ⓥ　搞砸，是種非正式的說法

screw-up Ⓝ

Have I screwed up the project?

我已經搞砸這案子了嗎？

 句型解析

You can rest assured that...「你可以放心，……」，表示確定事情發生會如所述般。常常使用的說法有"I am sure that…"或"I am certain that…"主詞是「我」，而"You can rest assured that…"主詞是「你」的用法。

句型延伸及範例

1. You are rest assured that the report will be on your desk tomorrow morning.

   您放心，明天早上這報告會在你的辦公桌上。

2. You can rest assured that Police will recover your wallet.

   你放心，警察會找到你的皮夾。

3. You may rest assured that your hardworking will not go in vain.

   你可以放心，你的努力不會徒勞無功。

 *MEMO*

It Goes Without Saying...

科技業無往不利的英語力

 **Dialogue**

John: Leila, may I talk to you?

Leila: Sure, what's up?

John: We have been invited by the customer to attend the opening ceremony next weekend in southern Taiwan. Some people on my team are not available to go, so I wonder if you would be interested in making the trip.

Leila: Well… let me check my calendar. I suppose I can move the weekend's activity to another day. Yes, I am able to go.

John: That's great. Of course, it **goes without saying** that all your travel expenses will be paid by the company.

Leila: May I know if I need to make a speech of any kind in the ceremony?

John: No. You just have to be there on behalf of the company.

對話譯文

John：Leila，我可以跟你商量一下嗎？

Leila：當然，什麼事？

John：我們收到客戶的邀請要參加他們週末在南台灣舉行的開幕儀式。我的團隊的一些人無法參加；因此，我在想是否你不介意去一趟。

Leila：嗯……讓我看看我的行程。我可以把週末的活動改到另一天，我想我能去。

John：太好了，當然不用説，所有的差旅費都由公司支付。

Leila：我想知道是否有要在儀式上致詞或説些話嗎？

John：不用，妳只需要代表公司出席。

 科技關鍵知識用語

1.**what's up?**　可以是問候語「還好嗎？」
　Hi, John. What's up?

嗨，John，還好嗎？

另外說法是問對方「什麼事嗎？」相同於"What's going on?"和
"Whats happening?"在這對話中的說法屬於後者「什麼事嗎？」

2. opening ceremony　開幕典禮

He will make a speech in the opening ceremony.

他將在開幕式上致辭。

"Grand opening" 則代表一個大樓或一個活動的開幕慶祝。
The Camera Club is ready for its grand opening and you're
invited! Enjoy big discounts on all our merchandise!

相機俱樂部準備好了盛大的開幕慶祝，邀請您來一同享受我們的所有商
品的大折扣！

3. make the trip　去一趟；跑一趟

I will be back from Australia by then. I should be able to
make the trip.

到時我會從澳洲回來，我應該能夠成行。

另外， "make a special trip" 意謂未在計畫中的行程，相當中文
「特別跑一趟」的意思。
Some local flights at the airport have been cancelled this
week. I will make a special trip by car to bring you the
shipment.

機場裡的一些地方航班這星期都已被取消。我會開車專程為你送這批
貨。

WEEK 3

科技業無往不利的英語力

句型解析

It goes without saying 不言而喻，不證自明，不用說……
用來說明事情是非常的明顯，不需多加解釋。這是一種禮貌方式帶出一些
已知道的知識的敘述。另外常說的用法有，"as you know"、"as we know"、"needless to say"或"of course"。

 句型延伸及範例

1.It goes without saying that you are able to communicate with foreign customers much easier if you improve your English fluency.

   如果你能夠讓你的英文更流暢的話，那不用說，你一定能更輕鬆地和外國客戶溝通。

2.Waiters in this country expect tips, as you know.

   你知道的，這國家的餐廳侍者是要給小費的。

3.Needless to say, our female sales reps can't do business in Dubai wearing the same clothes they did in Rio.

   不用說，我們在杜拜的女性業務員是不能穿得跟在里約熱內盧一樣服裝的。

4.Once we reach the airport, it goes without saying the immigration people will want to see our passports.

   一旦我們到達機場，不用說，移民局的人一定會要看我們的護照。

In Lieu of...

代替……

Dialogue

European Colleague: I heard in Taiwan you get nine days off in a row for Lunar New year. Wow, the company is so generous! In my country a New Year holiday usually lasts no more than three days.

Ms. Lee: Indeed, that is a wonderful way to arrange things. But we do take two of those vacation days **in lieu of** our personal leave. That's how we were able to make it nine days straight.

European Colleague: Nevertheless, it is superb. What's your plan for the holiday?

Ms. Lee: I have planned a family holiday in Japan. I am excited for it to come.

European Colleague: Japan is so picturesque. Enjoy your visit!

科技業無往不利的英語力

W E E K 3

In Lieu of...

 對話譯文

歐洲同事：我聽台灣這個中國新年假期你們有9天連續休假。哇，公司真是慷慨。在我的國家，我們的新年假期通常不會超過三天。

李女士：的確，這安排很棒。但其中有兩天是我們的私人休假來替代，這樣才有9天的連假。

歐洲同事：儘管如此，還是很棒。妳有何計劃？

李女士：我計劃一家人去日本度假，好期待喔！

歐洲同事：日本風景如畫，盡情享受吧！

 科技關鍵知識用語

1. in a row　連續

He has called in sick three days in a row. Do you know what's going on with him?

他連續三天打電話來請病假，你知道他是怎麼了嗎？

2. generous　adj　慷慨，大方，寬厚，夠意思

The restaurant is so generous! The size of each dish is not

small at all.

這餐廳真大方！每道菜都不小盤。

3. **9-days straight**　連續 9 天不間斷

This sales campaign will run for nine days straight.

這是連續九天的銷售活動。

4. **nevertheless**　儘管如此，雖然如此，不論如何

Nevertheless, he still got my vote.

儘管如此，他還是有我的選票。

5. **picturesque** adj 風景如畫

a. 視覺上的美麗

a picturesque old village（一座風景如畫的村莊）

b. 驚人的圖形或生動描述

a picturesque description of the Chinese bamboo garden（有關中國竹園栩栩如生的描述）

c. 有賞心悅目的或有趣的特質外觀

a picturesque hat（一頂賞心悅目的帽子）

句型解析

"**in lieu of**"「代替,替代,而不是……」,工作場所中通常用於休假的調動或彈性休假,**例如** 連假中的兩天是由個人年休假來補的情況下,則可以說"Two days in lieu of my annual leave."

另外常用的也有
★ payment in lieu–以付款代替。
★ payment in lieu of leave–假期折算的現金

例如

> For the balance of my annual leave entitlement, I request payment in lieu of time off.
>
> 我剩下的年假沒有休完,我向公司申請用現金代替。

 句型延伸及範例

1. For employees who resign, our company will reimburse the payment in lieu of last year's annual leave balance, with pro rata annual leave pay for the current leave year.

   對辭職員工,本公司將支付去年未休年假,今年年假按比例支付。

2. A restaurant that's run out of pumpkins might serve French onion soup in lieu of pumpkin soup.

   餐廳裡若南瓜用完,可能用法式洋蔥湯代替南瓜湯。

Come Up with

科技業無往不利的英語力

 **Dialogue**

A: The year-end party takes place soon. Did you know we have a tradition here? Every department is encouraged to **come up with** one program to perform at the party.

B: What did your team perform last year?

A: We didn't participate in the performance but this year we are planning to do some belly dancing. Five of my colleagues have been learning to dance. We are aiming for first place, with its reward of NT$100,000. The runner-up will get company products. That's not seen as a bonus at all.

B: Well…, to be honest, I am more interested in the lucky draw. I heard the first prize is a vacation voucher worth NT$100,000.

對話譯文

A：尾牙快到了，你知道我們有個傳統嗎？在尾牙時公司鼓勵每個部門進行一項表演。

B：那你們去年表演什麼？

A：去年我們沒有參加演出，但今年我們計劃表演肚皮舞，因為有五位同事學了一陣子了。而且，我們的目標是得第一名，可獲得新台幣 10 萬元的獎勵。亞軍只有獲得公司產品，那其實沒什麼意思。

B：嗯……，說實話，我對抽獎比較有興趣。聽說頭獎是個價值新台幣10萬元的假期兌換券。

 科技關鍵知識用語

1.take place　發生

A: When will this party take place?
B: It's taking place right now.

A：派對什麼時候開始？
B：現在就要開始！

2. aim at　針對，瞄準

The publicity campaign was aimed at improving the aviation safety.

這場宣傳活動是針對飛航安全。

還有"aim for"及"shoot for"，後者在語氣上有更具強烈野心之意。

We're aiming for a December date to open the new B&B.

我們準備在十二月，新的民宿要開始營業。

We're shooting for a new sales record this year.

我們今年要創業績新高峰。

3. first place　第一名

He won the first place in the marathon competition.

馬拉松比賽他得第一名。

4. reward　ⓥ　獎勵，激勵
rewarding　adj　值得的

The project has been very rewarding.

這個案子的結果相當值得。

5. runner up　第二名

The first-place act was incredible, and the runner-up also turned in a strong performance.

第一名的表演真是不可思議，而亞軍的表現也是很厲害。

6. worth　價值

Summer movies too often throw a hundred million dollars' worth of production at half a dollar's worth of story.

暑期的電影往往是花了價值上億美元來拍攝卻沒內容。

句型解析

"**Come up with**"往往有「創造出」、「原創」、「想出」的意思。不論是英文為母語的人或英文是第二語言的人,這都是很常見好用的說法。而 "come up with"除了上述的解釋之外,還有「追趕上」的意思。

例如

I had to run to come up with my cousin.

我得用跑的,才追趕上了我表哥。

 句型延伸及範例

1. By next year, the market for this product will be saturated. We will need to come up with some new ideas.

明年此產品的市場將達到飽和。我們需要想出一些新的辦法。

2. Let's see what he will come up with.

讓我們看看他會提出怎樣的主意。

You Don't Want to Do That!

你不會想這麼做的！

科技業無往不利的英語力

Dialogue

A: Hi, everyone. On the slide you see our production plan for the next two months. Due to insufficient supply, many common parts are on allocation. This has greatly impacted our fulfillment plan. As a result, the demand for model 3300 will only be 70% met in that time and model 3400 will be 50% met. We will be in receipt of more components in 60 days. Until then, this is all we can do.

B: **You don't want to do that!** We have commitment to fulfill the school tender with model 3400 as highlighted in our forecast spreadsheet. The fulfillment plan is not in alignment with our demand schedule. To align it more with our schedule, could you switch the product plan between those two models? Beside, we'd also like to explore if there is any way possible to meet 100% of the demand for model 3400. Any chance?

WEEK 3

You Don't Want to Do That!

 對話譯文

A： 嗨，大家好。你可以在投影片上看到這是在未來兩個月的生產計劃。由於供應不足，許多共用料有配額，這對生產計劃影響很大，因此我們只可以滿足型號 **3300** 百分之七十的需求，型號 **3400** 百分之五十。而下一次共用料進貨是 **60** 天後，在那之前，這是我們所有能生產的。

B： 你不會想這麼做！我們必須履行型號 **3400** 學校招標案的出貨，在我們的需求預估表中已有特別說明，你的生產計劃並不符合我們的出貨需求。為了更符合我們的計劃，可以調換這兩種型號的生產計劃嗎？除此之外，我們也想了解是否可能達成型號 **3400** 的百分之百出貨，有任何機會嗎？

科技關鍵知識用語

1. **allocation** n 分配
   allocate v 分配
   We need to determine the best way to allocate our resources.
   我們要決定最佳的方式來分配我們的資源。

2. **fulfillment** n 履行，滿足，完成
   fulfill v 履行，滿足，完成
   We have achieved 100% of order fulfillment.
   我們已經達成百分之百的訂單履行。

3. **in receipt of** 收到
   When we are in receipt of your money for the full balance, we will mark your bill as paid.
   當我們收到你的全額付款時，我們將會將你的帳單標示為已付款。

4. **in alignment with** 與…一致
   The company's results are in alignment with stock market expectations.
   公司的績效與股市期待一致。

5. **explore** v 探測，調查，探索
   Let us explore the meaning of this term.
   讓我們查一下這個詞的意義。

WEEK 3

科技業無往不利的英語力

句型解析

"You don't want to do that!"，意指你強烈的告訴對方不該這麼做，因為你認為那做法是錯的，相同於中文「你不會想這麼做」的說法。另外也可用進行式說法 "You don't want to be doing that!"，具有相同的意思，也常會聽到有人這麼說。

 句型延伸及範例

1. Eat before having any of that liquor from Kinmen. You do not want to be drinking that stuff on an empty stomach.

   在喝金門高粱飲前先吃點東西，你不會想空腹喝它的。

2. A: I am going to do product testing outdoors tomorrow.

   B: You don't want to do that! It is 90% chance of raining tomorrow.

   A：明天我將做產品戶外測試。

   B：你不會想這麼做！明天有 **90**％的機率會下雨。

He Can't
Help Himself...

他就是沒辦法⋯⋯

Dialogue

A: Gosh, his meeting drags! He rambles on and on and won't get into the point. My days are hectic with meetings lately. I am already late for the next one!

B: I think **he can't help himself.** You have to admit, though: he makes every effort to communicate. He takes care to make sure everyone takes part and understands responsibilities, so there is no communication gap.

A: That is very true. I have to run! Talk to you another day.

對話譯文

A：天哪，他的會議總是很會拖，説一大堆不知如何切入重點，我最近很忙，排滿了會議，我的下個會議已經開始了。

B：我覺得他就是沒辦法直接快一點，但你必須承認，他很盡力在溝通，讓每個人都了解所應負責的部分，不會有溝通斷層。

A：這倒是真的。我要走了！改天再跟你聊。

科技關鍵知識用語

1.**drag** Ⅴ 拖延，拖著
He dragged his tired feet slowly along.
他拖着疲倦的步伐慢慢地走着。

2.**hectic** adj 忙碌的
She lives a hectic business schedule period.
她過著繁忙的商務排程生活。

另外還有一個可以用來形容行程很滿的説法"**wall-to-wall**"，中文為「填滿」的意思。這一個字原本是用來形容一個房間裡的地毯從這一邊的牆鋪到另一邊的牆，鋪滿了整個房間，之後則被延伸來形容「滿」的這一個狀態，例如是在房間裡擠滿了人，可以說是"wall-to-wall people"，而用來形容繁忙的工作行程，則可參考下面的例句。

My days are wall-to-wall with meetings!

我每天有開不完的會。

3. take part 　參與

She does not take part in the conversation.

她沒加入談話。

4. communication gap 　溝通斷層

This is one way to break the communication gap between parents and children.

這是一個打破親子間溝通斷層的一個方式。

5. I have to run 　我要走了

這說法有點在趕時間的意味，而 I have to go 則是簡單的說我要走了。

 句型解析

當聽到有人說"he can't help himself"，其實並不是如字面上的意思他沒辦法幫助他自己，其實正確意思是他無法抗拒做一些事。可能是對某些事的誘惑無法抗拒，也可以是個性上的問題造成習慣性的行為舉止。

譬如，你每天喝很多的茶飲，而當你的朋友問你為何喝這麼多茶飲料，你可能只是簡單地回答"I just can't help myself!"，代表這是你的習慣，就是無法拒絕。

句型延伸及範例

1.A: Why does she keep giggling while she talks?

B: She can't help herself.

A：她說話時為什麼不斷地傻笑？

B：她就是這樣。

2.I just can't help myself not to think about her after we broke up.

我們分手後，我就是沒辦法不去想她。

You May Want to...

你可能要……

科技業無往不利的英語力

 **Dialogue**

A: May I talk to you for some advices?

B: Sure. Shoot.

A: I have received a gift from the supplier. The gift is quite valuable, and I am sure it is intended only as a polite gesture, but I am concerned about ethics. Last week, we have discovered design flaws in their components that we procured. Now this.

B: Indeed. We have been seeing quite a few scandals in the industry lately. The gift could be interpreted as a bribe. **You may want to** return it and report the whole thing to your supervisor. Whatever happens, you want to establish your own integrity.

 對話譯文

A： 我可以和你談一下聽聽你的建議嗎？

B： 當然，説吧。

A： 我收到供應商送來的禮物。禮品價值不菲，我相信這是供應商禮貌性的動作，但我擔心道德原則。上星期我們發現向供應商採購的元件中有設計缺陷。現在又是這個。

B： 的確。最近在業界，有不少受賄醜聞，你收到禮物可能被看成是一種賄賂。你可能要退回禮物，同時向你的主管報告，不管如何你會想要建立你的誠信。

科技關鍵知識用語

1. shoot ⓥ 射擊，發出
   一般用法是射擊或發射，但在非常口語對話上，表示「説出來吧」或「説吧」。

2. gesture ⓝ 姿勢，手勢，儀態，舉止
   She kept me aloof by reserved gesture.
   她對我的態度很矜持，敬而遠之。

科技業無往不利的英語力

3. **ethic** n 道德／**ethical** adj 合乎道德

He has always prided himself on being honest and ethical.

他一直為自己為人正派、做事公道感到自豪。

4. **design flaws** 設計瑕疵／**flawless** 完美無瑕[=perfect]

Everything seems to be in flawless working condition.

所有的看起來都完美無瑕。

5. **indeed** adv 的確。用於強烈的認同一件事或一個觀點。

He is indeed an honest man.

他的確是個誠實的人。

6. **scandal** n 醜聞，丟臉的事件，舞弊案件

The matter will be a scandal once it gets out.

這件事情說出去會是丟臉的事。

7. **bribe** n 行賄，賄賂／**bribery** n ／**to bribe** v

He was charged with bribery.

他被指控受賄。

She offered me a bribe to forget the whole matter rather than report it.

她賄賂我要我忘記整件事，不要呈報。

He was bribed. The supplier was giving him kickbacks for every order our company made.

他被賄賂，供應商給他我們公司每一筆訂單的回扣。

8. **integrity** n 誠信，廉正

I'm not questioning their integrity at all.

我對他們的廉正無私沒有任何質疑。

句型解析

"**you may want to...**" 中文為「你可能要……」，這是一種禮貌的方式讓對方知道該採取的正確行動，當是主管或是較有權威者對你說 "**you may want to**…"時，與其說是建議不如說是個命令，而當事同儕或朋友對你說時表示強烈建議該採取的行動。

另外常用說法 "**you may as well**…"「你最好……」，用以表示應該沒有其他更好的方式。

例如

You may want to take the bus home. 你可能要搭公車回家。
You may as well take the bus home. 你最好搭公車回家。

 句型延伸及範例

1. The snow storm is coming and the airport will be closed. You may want to stay in town overnight.
   冰風暴即將來臨，機場將被關閉。你可能要留在鎮上過夜。

2. You may want to inform your family about the late departure of your plane.
   您可能要通知您的家人你的飛機會誤點。

3. You may want to explain to the whole team for the reason of changing schedule.
   您可能要解釋給整個團隊知道時程改變的原因。

Having Said That...

話雖如此……

科技業無往不利的英語力

 **Dialogue**

Sales Manager: Bad news: our whole batch of products failed in the French market. Given confirmation with the authorities, we know this is an epidemic failure. We have to recall each and every item, whether sold or still stocked in the customers' warehouse.

Boss: Have we identified the source of the problem at our end?

Sales Manager: Yes, we have. The product team has re-constructed the problem at our end and confirmed that the root cause lies in design flaws.

Boss: This is our second product failure in a year. I will have to review the performance of the entire product team. **Having said that,** I feel our sales team also bears some responsibility here. Sales reps could have taken immediate action when the customer first reported the issue a month ago. Fewer flawed devices would have been sold, resulting in less damage to our market.

88

W
E
E
K
3

Having Said That...

 對話譯文

業務經理：有個壞消息，我們的整批產品在法國市場有產品瑕疵。根據相關單位確定，這是設計缺陷，不論已售出的還是仍在客戶倉庫中的，我們必須整批回收。

老闆：我們是否已證實了問題呢？

業務經理：是的，產品團隊已在我們這裡重建問題確認根本原因是設計瑕疵造成。

老闆：這已是一年內第二次產品問題。我得仔細評估整個產品團隊的問題。話雖如此，業務團隊也有責任應該在客戶一個月前首次通報問題時就採取行動，越少產品流到市上，可減少所造成的傷害。

科技關鍵知識用語

1. epidemic failure　產品設計瑕疵

According to the contract, the vendor has to recall all the products at its own expense in the event of an epidemic failure.

根據合約規定，當有產品設計瑕疵時，供應商必須負責所有費用回收所有產品。

2. recall　Ⅴ　召回，回想

We have decided to recall all the products sold in this market.

我們決定回收所有售出至市場上的產品。

3. at our end　在我們這端

★ at your end　在你那邊
★ at customer's end　在客戶端
★ at the other end　在另一端

How is everything at your end?

你那邊還好嗎？

 句型解析

"**Having said that**"（話雖如此，雖然這麼説）是一種轉換語氣，代表即將説的主題與前面説的主題相反或有不同的意見。這是口語上很常用的説法，也是很好用的語句。

另外可取代的用法是"**that said**"，和"**with that said**"。

例如

The place is so beautiful. Having said that, I have many other places to see in this trip.

The place is so beautiful. That said, there are so many beautiful places we have yet to visit in this trip.

這地方真美，話雖如此，這一趟，我還有很多其他地方沒去。

The place is so beautiful. With that said, there are many other places to see.

這個地方好漂亮。這樣一說，有許多的地方值得看看。

 句型延伸及範例

1. This customer complained about our new product. Having said that, they have placed a big order.

   這個客戶對我們的新產品有所抱怨。話雖如此，他們還是下了一個大訂單。

2. The colors in this painting are so vivid! That said, you can still do more with your brushwork.

   在這幅畫的顏色是如此生動。話雖如此，你的筆觸仍有改善的空間。

The Bottom Line Is...

關鍵在於，最終的考量……

科技業無往不利的英語力

 **Dialogue**

A: Hi, colleagues. It's that time of year again with our company's overseas outing right around the corner. I would like to hear your ideas about where we can go and what we can do.

B: In view of the Japanese currency drop, the time is right to visit Japan. We can more easily afford the trip this year.

C: Given how cold it is now in Taipei, I think we would all appreciate the lovely warmth of a Southeast Asian countries.

CEO: It has been a tough year but, thanks to all the hard work by our employees, we have managed to maintain a very healthy financial status. As a reward I am happy to send the whole team on a trip we will all enjoy. I am sure everyone can suggest fun places. Keep in mind, though, that **our bottom line has** to be safety.

 對話譯文

A： 大家好。很快又是公司海外之旅，我希望能聽聽大家的建議，看今年我們想去哪裡，做什麼活動。

B： 由於日元匯率的下滑，今年去日本將比以前省下更多費用，我認為這是一個很好的時機去日本。

C： 我想台北最近這麼冷，大家應該會很感謝能去東南亞國家享受溫暖。

CEO： 這是一個艱難的一年，但透過大家的努力，我們的營收狀況仍能保持得相當穩健。為了獎勵大家，我希望大家都能好好享受出國之旅。不管你們的建議是什麼，我相信都是好玩的地方。但是，我希望提醒一點，無論最後決定去哪裡，我們最終考量是安全性。

科技關鍵知識用語

1. In view of 考慮到；由於

In view of the high cost of gasoline, I take MRT to work.

由於汽油的成本很高，我坐地鐵上班。

2. The time is right to… / It would be good timing to…
正是時候

The time is right to look for a new job after lunar New Year.

過農曆年後正是找新工作的好時機。

3. keep in mind 記住

Please keep in mind: you job is to manage people, instead of doing everything yourself.

請記住：你的工作是去管理人，而不是自己做一切的工作。

 句型解析

"**the bottom line…**"是用來結束一段對話，或是做最後的說明和總結，通常也是想提出自己認為最重要的考量，希望別人能加以思考的內容。

用於財務說明時，bottom line 則是財務最後的 P&L (Profit and Loss Statement)結果，也就是帳目盈虧的結算結果。

科技業無往不利的英語力

句型延伸及範例

1. If our flight is late, we will miss our connection. That's the bottom line.

   如果我們的飛機晚點，我們會錯過轉機，這是最終結果。

2. The bottom line is that we have to complete the task by Friday.

   最終的底線是：我們必須在週五前完成任務。

3. The bottom line will always be the cost.

   成本永遠是最終考量。

All Things Being Equal...

如果事情進行順利的話……

Dialogue

A: Hello, all. I am here today to update all of you about the preparations for our press conference. I will just run though the slides quickly: (1) the date, (2) the venue, (3) the theme, (4) the list of media invited, (5) the guest list, (6) the agenda, and (7) the duty roster.
A busy news day can always depress turnout for a presser, naturally, but **all things being equal** we can expect around 50 journalists.

B: The preparations look great. Is the press release ready? When can we send it out?

A: The final version of the release text is being reviewed today by management. The release date has yet to be confirmed. We will keep you up-to-date on that.

💬 **對話譯文**

A：大家好，今天我在這裡為大家說明這次新產品發表會的媒體招待會目前準備內容。我將很快地說明簡報內容：1）日期、2）場地、3）主題、4）媒體邀請名單、5）嘉賓名單、6）議程、7）員工排班表。當天如有太多其他新聞會影響媒體出席率，如果事情順利進行，沒有意外的話，我們可以期待大約 50 個新聞媒體前來。

B：內容看起來準備很充分。那我們的新聞稿是否準備就緒？以及什麼時候可以發送出去呢？

A：新聞稿正在等主管們的批准。發布日期會再確認，到時會讓大家知道。

1. venue Ⓝ 地點〔一個事件或活動發生的地點〕

There has been a change of venue for the rehearsal.

排練的場地已經改地方了。

2. duty roster 值班表

Please refer to the duty roster of running our booth in the exhibition.

請參考我們在展覽中的展攤位管理值班表。

3. a busy news day 指當天（社會上）有許多可報導的新聞

Geez, it has been a busy news day. I didn't even have time to eat dinner.

我的天啊，今天的新聞多到不行。我甚至沒空吃晚餐。

4. turnout Ⓝ 參與人數

The marathon in the east coast attracted a large turnout.

東海岸的馬拉松賽吸引許多參賽者。

WEEK 4

科技業無往不利的英語力

句型解析

"**All things being equal...**"在這個對話中指的是「如果事情進行順利的話……」。其用法如下,而不同用法的例句請參考句型延伸。

1. 當事情如預期般發展時的情況。

2. 如果情況沒改變,沒有其他複雜因子的加入。

3. 但另外稍微不同的説法還有,當所有其他變數皆相同時。

 句型延伸及範例

1. We could always find ourselves running into some problems in the final meeting, but all things being equal I should be home by this weekend.

   在最後的會議中,總是會有些問題,但如果一切順利,我在週末前會回到家。

2. All things being equal, we should have no trouble getting your order to you on time.

   沒有其他意外的話,你的訂單我們應該可準時交貨。

3. All things being equal, I prefer the rounded table.

   當所有條件皆相同時,我比較喜圓桌。

Tell Me About It!

科技業無往不利的英語力

 **Dialogue**

A: Which brand of smartphone are you using?

B: I am using the phone we made, of course.

A: One bonus when you work for a smartphone company is that you get free phones. It has been years since I spent my own money to purchase one. But, look at this handset made by our competitor. It is so easy to use and the quality is terrific. Our phone can't compare in terms of user experience.

B: **Tell me about it!** I like their products, too, even though they are our competitor.

對話譯文

A： 你用哪個品牌的智慧型手機？

B： 我當然是用我們公司自己生產的。

A： 在智慧型手機的公司工作的其中一個獎勵就是有免費的手機可用，已經很多年我沒花錢買手機。但是你看看這個，我們競爭對手生產的智慧型手機，很容易操作，品質又無話可說。講到用戶體驗，我們的手機是沒得比。

B： 不用你說，雖然它是我們的競爭對手，但我喜歡他們的產品。

科技關鍵知識用語

1.**bonus** 🅝 獎金，獎勵，意外的禮物，奉送品

不單單是與金錢有關的獎勵，也可用於描述在某情況下意外的贈品

Being upgraded to Business Class is a bonus for the trip.

升級到商務艙是此行的意外禮物。

2.**user experience** 用戶體驗

What's the difference in user experience between Apple and Samsung?

蘋果和三星間的用戶體驗有什麼不同？

  句型解析

"**Tell me about it!**"它的解釋完全與字面意思不同，它的真正意思是「你不說我也知道」、「我知道你在說什麼，我也有相同的經驗」或是「我完全同意你的意見」。有時，也用來回答你對某人所經歷的問題或不好的經驗感到同情。

"**Tell me about it!**"是非常口語化的說法，適當的用在對話當中，會讓你聽起來更平易近人。

1. A: What a rough day.
   B: Tell me about it."

   A：好辛苦的一天啊。

   B：可不是嘛。

   對英文為第二語言的人來說，可能會問為什麼 "Tell me about it." 與字面的意思完全不同，語言有時不能問為什麼，只有不斷學習和練習，將學到的應用在工作上，就會成為自己的了。

2. A: I love our friend, Mary, but she can be a real bother sometimes.
   B: Oh, tell me about it.

   A：我愛我們的朋友，瑪麗，但她有時還真讓人頭痛。

   B：哦，不用你說。

3. A: I've got so much work to do.
   B: Tell me about it!

   A：我有這麼多的工作要做。

   B：我知道，我也是！

4. A: He's driving me crazy with his attitude.
   B: Tell me about it!

   A：他的態度快把我逼瘋了。

   B：深有同感！

To Put Sth. Into Perspective

用更長遠的眼光來看

 **Dialogue**

A: The competition in this industry is getting fierce. It's a cutthroat business these days. The prices have dropped quickly, but with no compromise in product specs or performance. Being a small player in the market, we face the crucial question of how to survive.

B: I heard we will be merged into ABC Company.

A: That wouldn't be good. Many of us would be out of work. I've heard stories about how ABC Company manages its R&D team. I don't want to be a part of it.

B: It is actually not a bad idea, if you **put it into perspective**. We will have more resources and can more easily achieve a state-of-the-art product.

科技業無往不利的英語力

 對話譯文

A：這個行業競爭越來越激烈，簡直是個割喉市場了。價格掉的如此之快，但產品的規格和性能沒有妥協。作為市場的小咖，我們面臨著如何生存下去的關鍵點。

B：我聽說，我們要被併到 ABC 公司。

A：糟糕透了，很多人會因此失去工作，我有聽說 ABC 公司如何管理研發團隊，我不喜歡那樣的方式。

B：如果換個角度用更長遠的眼光來看，這其實並不是一件壞事。我們將有更多的資源來開發更先進的產品。

科技關鍵知識用語

1. **fierce**　adj　殘忍的，凶猛的，猛烈的，多用以形容戰爭或競爭的激烈或殘忍
We got ready for a fierce battle.
我們準備進行一場惡戰。

Competition was growing fiercer every year.

競爭一年比一年激烈。

The tiger is a fierce animal.

老虎是一種兇猛的動物。

2. **cutthroat** n adj 割喉；割喉般激烈（特指在競爭上的激烈）

It reflects the cutthroat competition in the current market.

它反應出了在目前市場上的激烈競爭。

3. **compromise** n v 妥協，調和，和解

They reached a compromise the same day.

在那一天，他們達成妥協。

Our principle is not to compromise on safety.

我們的原則是安全沒有妥協。

4. **merge** v 吞沒，使消失（在……中）(in; into)，合併，併入

We would like to merge the two teams into one.

我們要將兩隊合併為一。

The sky and the water seem to merge at the far end.

在遙遠處水天連一線。

另外商場上常聽到的企業併購則是merger and acquisition（併購）。

5. **state-of-the-art** n 尖端科技

The device uses state-of-the-art technology to achieve impressive results.

這裝置採用所有最新的技術達到驚人的結果。

句型解析

To put sth. into perspective...意思是以更大的格局及角度來看目前遇到的情況及問題，也傳遞了訊息你對這整件事的了解，也讓其他人知道以不同角度看這件事的重要性。短短的幾個字不需太多贅述，但卻提醒他人以許多不同的思維方式來多方考慮。

句型延伸及範例

1. You might think it is an extra burden in study for children to learn more languages in school. But to put it into perspective, children can have more language skills.

   你可能會認為讓孩子們在學校學多種語言是額外的學習負擔。但以更大的角度來看，孩子們可以有更多的語言能力。

2. To put it into perspective, to pay more income tax will allow the country to improve its infrastructure.

   以長遠的角度來看，付更多的所得稅可讓這國家改善它的基礎設施。

I Don't Buy It!

科技業無往不利的英語力

我不相信！

 **Dialogue**

Account Manager: I got a call from our customer in Prague. They wonder if we can release the shipment today on their promise to make the remaining payment tomorrow.

Boss: <u>I don't buy it!</u> That customer has a history of late payment.

Account Manager: They didn't keep their promise on the date a couple of times. On the other hand, they've always paid. Given them credit for that. We can't deny their potential for our business in the Czech Republic. They are hoping we will do them the favor of releasing the shipment today so they can catch the seasonal sales. It's a small overdue amount, so the financial exposure for us is also relatively small.

108

對話譯文

客戶經理：我接到捷克布拉格客戶打來的電話，他們答應明天會付貨物餘款，看我們今天是否能出貨。

老闆：我不相信！這客戶有付款不準時的紀錄。

客戶經理：他們有兩次沒信守承諾準時付款，但他們最後還是有付，而我們不能否認他們對我們在捷克的業務拓展上非常有潛力。他們希望我們能幫忙同意今天放貨，好趕上這季節促銷。這未付款項金額很小，對我們而言沒有太大的財務風險。

 科技關鍵知識用語

1. make payment 付款

When can you expect to make payment?

你何時會付款？

★ make a payment 付貸款(pay one installment)
★ pay in full 付清(pay the complete amount)

2. **credit** n v 信用，信任，名譽

是個在工作上常用到的字，值得多加學習與注意。

a. I never gave you enough credit for your skill.

我沒想到你有這個能力。

b. I cannot take credit for this success. It was a team effort.

這是團隊的努力，我不能承攬成功的功勞。

c. credit account 信用帳戶

The rates are applicable to credit account customers only.

這優惠利率只限於信用帳戶之客戶。

d. open credit 信用貸款；信用往來

We have to reassure our support to the customer by offering favorable open credit terms.

提供優惠的公開授信條件，對我們的客戶表示支持。

e. credit line 可用信用限額

Your available credit line limit is written in the Contract.

你可用的信用額度如合約中所述。

3. **overdue** adj 逾期

The library called in all overdue books.

圖書館要求把所有逾借書收回。

4. **financial exposure** 財務風險

In view of the amount, our financial exposure is low.

以這金額來看，我們的財務風險是低的。

句型解析

I don't buy it! 意思是「我不相信！」，所提及的人或單位過去曾發生不遵守諾言的情況，或是你被告知某個消息，你不相信時所回答的方式。與 "I don't believe it!"是相同的意思，只是更口語化。

 句型延伸及範例

1. They said the authority will reduce the energy price. I don't buy it!

   他們說有關當局會降低能源價格，我不相信！

2. Someone told me all the employees will get a 5% salary increase. I'm not buying it.

   有人說我們所有的員工都會有 5 ％的加薪，我才不信！

3. A: Why did John get fired?

   B: I heard he accepted a bribe from the supplier.

   A: I don't buy that. I have known John for more than 10 years and he is the most honest person I know.

   A：約翰為什麼被解僱？

   B：我聽說他接受供應商賄賂。

   A：我不相信！我認識他已經有超過 10 年了，他是我認識的人中最誠實的人。

It Doesn't Hurt to...

 **Dialogue**

A: You look very frustrated.

B: Yes, I'm facing time pressure. I need to confirm with our supplier how best to proceed so as to kick off production. It's critical if we're to fulfill the orders from customers.

A: You have mentioned that one week ago, still pending?

B: Yes, the agreement is still on the boss's desk. She seems extremely busy lately. She has not much time at her desk.

A: If the production kick-off is so critical, it doesn't hurt to send her a reminder through email.

科技業無往不利的英語力

112

 對話譯文

A：你看起來很沮喪。

B：是啊，我有時間壓力，必須趕快與供應商確認如何開始進行生產，而這批生產對滿足客戶訂單是關鍵。

A：一個星期前你不是就在進行了嗎？仍懸而未決？

B：嗯，合約仍在老闆的辦公桌上，她似乎非常忙，最近沒太多的時間坐在辦公室。

A：如果開始生產如此重要，送個郵件來提醒你的老闆也無妨。

科技關鍵知識用語

1.frustrate　v　失敗，受挫折

I find it frustrating that I can't identify the root cause. .

找不到問題根源，讓我感到很沮喪。

2.proceed　v　前進；邁進；出發，開始，著手

這是個在工作場所很好用的字，簡簡單單一個字代表許多含意。

How to proceed?

如何進行？如何繼續？如何開始？如何下一步邁進？

在許多不同情況下，這個字都可使用。

3.pending　adj　未決，待決

The decision is still pending.

仍未下決定。

 句型解析

當有人告訴你 **"it doesn't hurt to do something"**，並不是如字面意思「做這件事你不會感到痛」，其實是要告訴你這麼做實在是對你有利，值得一試，做了對你有利無害。

這句也是非常口語的說法，對英文是第二語言的人來說，若不用這句話，可能要用很長一句話才能表同樣的意思。

句型延伸及範例

1. It doesn't hurt to do it again and see if you can find a more efficient way to do.

   不妨再做一遍，看看你是否能找到一種更有效的方式。

2. It doesn't hurt to have more people join the game, if you want more media exposure.

   如果你要更多的媒體曝光，有更多的人加入這比賽沒有不好。

3. It doesn't hurt to wait for one more day before you move on.

   你不妨再多等一天再出發。

 MEMO

How Do You Find...?

你對……覺得怎麼樣？

科技業無往不利的英語力

 **Dialogue**

A: How was your flight? Thanks for coming all the way over here to help us with the product issues.

B: My flight was pleasant. I am happy to help. I reviewed the document and report on the way here. I have some more ideas of how to proceed.

A: That's great. First time here, <u>how do you find</u> this country so far?

B: I only get to see the airport and so far, it is nice.

A: Let's check you into the hotel and settle in first. Later, we go for dinner. Rest well tonight. We have a long week ahead of us.

 對話譯文

A： 你的這一趟飛行旅程還好嗎？謝謝你大老遠趕來這裡幫忙解決我們的產品問題。

B： 我的旅程還好。我很樂意能夠幫忙，在飛行中我看了一些文件及報告，我有一些想法如何進行。

A： 那太好了。你第一次來，對這國家感覺如何？

B： 目前只看到機場，都還不錯。

A： 讓你先入住旅館，休息一下。晚點，我們去吃飯。你今天好好休息，我們將有忙碌的一週。

 科技關鍵知識用語

1.come all the way　大老遠，一路過來

Do you come all the way here just to bring me my books?

你大老遠跑過來只是把我的書拿給我嗎？

2.rest well　好好休息

Rest well and good night.

117

好好休息，晚安。

3. **settle in** （使）安頓下來；適應新環境（工作）

She seems to have settled in very well at her new company.

她在新公司似乎適應得很好。

4. **ahead of us** 我們眼前

It is a tough journey ahead of us.

眼前的路是很艱辛的。

 句型解析

當有人問你 "**How do you find** your job?" 不要一股腦地回答你是如何找到這份工作。他問的是「你對你的工作感覺如何？」。若是問如何找到這工作，說法應該是 "How did you get this job?" or "How did you find your job?"

"How do you find your job?" 的可替代的說法為 "What do you think about your job?"。

1. How do you find your new house?

   你喜歡妳的新家嗎？

2. How do you find your new iPhone?

   你的新 iPhone 怎麼樣？

   （特指詢問對方新的 iPhone 好不好用，喜歡與否？）

MEMO

In My Defense, ...

我要辯解的是⋯⋯

Dialogue

科技業無往不利的英語力

Project Leader: Earlier I expressed my disappointment about missing the project's completion schedule. Today, I would like to learn the reasons for the delay.

Hardware Manager: I can share details from the hardware point of view. We have managed to stick to the schedule and are at the final stage of making minor modifications, such as color fine-tuning. We have had to change the antenna a few times but that is not the cause of the project delay.

Project Leader: How about software team?

Software Manager: I have to admit that some of the delay is due to software readiness. **In my defense**, the original projections were based on past experience and progress. The complexity of the device is actually unprecedented in our product history. One of the engineers also had to take a week off at a crucial point due to a personal emergency.

W
E
E
K
5

In My Defense, ...

Project: Thanks to you both for your efforts on this project.
Leader This is not to challenge any member or complain about any team. Our goal is to identify the issues and address them.

 對話譯文

專案負責人：早先我提過對案子的進度落後感到失望，今天我想知道是什麼原因造成延誤。

硬體經理：從硬體的角度來分享一些情況，我們都照時間表在走，目前在最後的細微修改，如顏色的微調。雖然天線改了幾次，但並沒有造成任何延誤。

專案負責人：軟體部份呢？

軟體經理：我承認有些因為軟體而引起的延遲。但我必須解釋，原先對這些案子的評估是以過去經驗來研判，這產品的複雜性超過我們過去所做的，再加上有位工程師因個人因素在重要時間點請假一星期。

121

專案負責人：感謝兩個團隊在這個案子上的努力，今天不是在責備任何成員或抱怨任何團隊，只是要找出問題且如何解決。

 科技關鍵知識用語

1. express
v 表達（文字或肢體語言表達一個想法或感覺）
adj 快速（例如，express train）

I have expressed my opinion by walking out of the room without saying anything. That should be clear to everyone.

我已經以不發一語就走出房間的舉動來表達我的意見，大家應該都明白。

2. stick to
堅持；信守；粘在…上；遵守

That is my story and I am sticking to it.

我說的就是這些，不會改變。

The piece of paper stuck to my fingers.

這紙片粘在我的手指上了。

3. admit
v 承認，接受，許可入場

I freely admit that I made a mistake.

我欣然承認我犯了個錯誤。

當說"I must admit"則有另外的意思，暗示雖然承認但有點不如所想的。

I didn't expect to enjoy the presentation, but I must admit I learned a lot.

我沒預期會喜歡這次的簡報，但我必須承認，我學到了很多東西。

Our competitor's design team does an outstanding job, I

科技業無往不利的英語力

must admit.

我必須承認我們公司的設計團隊表現很優異。

4. go beyond 超過

What I am going to present goes way beyond your imagination.

我將要呈現的遠超過你的想像。

 句型解析

"In my defense" 通常用來合理化事情發生的原因或所做決定的結果，尤其當結果不是一個大家期待的結果，或是事情進行不如預期的情況下。在工作場合中常會用到，尤其在一些爭執或覺得自己被攻擊需要爭取一個合理立場來解釋事情發生原因時。這也是在法庭中的用法，為自己抗辯一個合理立場。

 句型延伸及範例

1. The only thing I can say in my defense is that I was extremely busy during the summer working on my new house.

我唯一可辯解的是，我整個夏天都非常忙著整理我的新房子。

2. In my defense, I didn't know the child was sleeping in one of the rooms in the house before I locked it off.

我要辯解的是，在我鎖上房子前，我不知道孩子還睡在其中一個房間裡。

Let's Get Down to Business...

讓我們進入正題……

 **Dialogue**

科技業無往不利的英語力

Jason and Cecilia are from Company XYZ.

Jason: This is an innovation: the first wearable device that allows you to operate your smartphone using gestures from your hands and arms .

Cecelia: Yes. For instance, when there is an incoming call, you can easily answer it with a simple gesture that you have already taught the device to recognize. There are 10 features we have allocated for your preference.

Jason: You are the first customer we have presented this innovation to. That shows the interest we have in doing business with your company.

Customer: So far, it sounds amazing. **Let's get down to the business.** We can sign an MOU for further confidential information disclosure.

WEEK 5

Let's Get Down to Business...

 對話譯文

Jason 和 Cecilia 都來自 XYZ 公司。

Jason：這是這個產業的創新產品，第一個可穿戴的裝置能夠透過手勢來操作你的智能手機。

Cecilia：是的，例如當有來電時，你可以很容易地通過你已經輸入到設備中的特定手勢來回答你的電話。還有，可依您的喜好有 10 個功能可供選擇。

Jason：貴公司是我們展示這創新產品的第一個客戶，這證明我們有極高的興趣與貴公司合作。

客戶：到目前為止，這聽起來很棒。讓我們進入正題，我們可以先簽一個 MOU 來進一步揭露機密資訊。

科技關鍵知識用語

1. gesture　n　姿勢，姿態，手勢

在科技產業中，由於無線傳輸產品的盛行，藉由手勢來操作儀器，gesture 變成常看到的字。

Follow the gestures written in the instructions to operate the device.

請參照操作手冊中所寫的手勢來操作這裝置。

2. designated　adj　特定，指定

He is designated person to sign the contract.

他被指定來簽署這一份合約。

3. MOU 備忘錄 (Memorandum of Understanding)

MOU 在初期階段所簽訂的國際契約，對每一方的參與表達對此議題某程度的嚴肅性，接下來會簽定正式合約。通常除非在內容有特殊規範，否則在法律上無法律約束。

If all parties here are interested in doing business, we can draft an MOU for everyone to sign.

如果在這裡的所有團體對這生意都有興趣的話，我們可以準備一份備忘錄讓大家簽。

4. disclosure　n　揭發；公佈

Disclosure of additional information in the reports will expedite the process.

在報告中披露的其他信息將加快處理進度。

句型解析

<u>"Let's get down to business"</u> 是一種說法結束目前的對話來進入嚴肅的討論主題。 這些對話可能是（例如）產品介紹，一連串的談判，亦或是無關緊要的對話，**"let's get down to business"** 將整個談話內容帶入另一層次的主題。

 句型延伸及範例

1. OK, let's let stop the banter and get down to business.

   好了，讓我們停止所有的玩笑，談談正事。

2. Your product introduction sounds great. Now let's get down to business. What price can you offer?

   你的產品介紹聽起來很不錯，現在讓我們言歸正傳，你的價格是什麼 ？

3. After weeks of discussion and factory visits, the customer finally got down to business and agreed to a contract.

   經過幾星期的討論和工廠參觀，客戶最後終於回到正題並決定在合同上簽字。

Correct Me If I'm Wrong...

如果有不對的地方，請告訴我

科技業無往不利的英語力

 **Dialogue**

A: I am going to recap our discussion. Please <u>correct me if I am wrong</u>. The following is our mutual understanding as we move forward:

(1) The project will promote green technology by placing demonstration sites in bicycle rental stations around the Taipei City;

(2) Both parties agree to promote and market the project via special events and media material.

B: Thank you for the summary. Could you please put this into an email and send it to all the participants in the meeting today?

🗨️❗ **對話譯文**

A： 我來重複一下我們的討論，如果有不對的地方，請告訴我。下面是我們的共識：

1）這案子設置將是在台北市的自行車租賃站作為示範點來促進綠能技術;

2）為了推動這案子，雙方同意安排行銷活動來表示彼此的對此案的投入。

B：謝謝你的總結。能否請您用電子郵件將內容送給今天所有的參與者？

 科技關鍵知識用語

1. recap ⓝ/ⓥ 重述要點

I'd like to do a quick recap of the idea about the target audience of what we have identified.

我在此快速地回顧一下有關我們已經確定的目標觀眾的想法。

In the few minutes we have left, I want to recap the main points that were made today.

在剩下來的幾分鐘，我想回顧一下今天的要點。

At the top of the sports news tonight, a packed arena at the World Cup watched a thrilling match today between Ivory Coast and Portugal. Here's a recap of the action.

在體育新聞今晚的頭條，今天在世界杯賽場上擠滿觀看象牙海岸對葡萄

129

牙的一場驚心動魄的比賽。這裡是今天的回顧。

2. move forward 向前進

This report helps us to get the big picture about where we stand and what sorts of choices we face as we move forward.

此報告有助於有我們能用較大的角度來審視我們的處境和在走下一步時我們有哪些選擇。

3. mutual understanding 共識

I am glad we've reached a mutual understanding about this project that lets us see better how to proceed.

很高興我們對這案子的共識，讓我們更清楚如何進行。

4. address Ⓥ 載明

The presenter plays a key role in delivering information that addresses customers' expectations.

這簡報者在傳達客戶預期的資訊上，扮演了一個關鍵的角色。

 句型解析

"Correct me if I'm wrong" 是一種禮貌的說法來強調你想做的陳述，尤其是你很確定，但還是禮貌地給予對方更正的空間，用 "Correct me if I am wrong" 來開始句子。另外類似的說法 "If I am not mistaken…"，兩者有相同的功用和意思。

1. Please correct me if I am wrong, as I know the product design you just proposed will soon be updated within a three months' timeframe.

   如果我説的不對，請告訴我，我知道你剛才提出的產品設計的新版本將在 3 個月內出來。

2. Please correct me if I am wrong. If I am not mistaken, you agree to postpone the product launch date for another two months so that we can have the chance to improve the product performance.

   如果我説的不對，請告訴我，如果我沒搞錯，您同意將產品上市時間延後兩個月，這樣我們就可以有機會提高產品性能。

3. If I am not mistaken, you are planning to invest in our project.

   如果我沒有聽錯，你打算投資於我們的案子。

Run the Risk of...

冒……的風險

 **Dialogue**

A: In this meeting, we are to finalize the product spec. In order to widen our product portfolio, we are aiming to offer a product at the low end with the street price at NT$4,000, which means the product cost has to be within US$40.

B: We fully understood the reason for coming out with a budget device. However, I would like to raise one concern. We are **running the risk of** not being able to meet Android compatibility requirements if we don't increase the speed of the processor and the built-in memory size. Users will have problems running most aftermarket applications.

A: Your point is taken. Let's go through all the details and redo the assessment.

對話譯文

A： 今天的會議我們要確定最終的產品規格。為了擴大我們的產品線,目標是做出一個產品零售價在台幣四千元,也就是說成本必須控制在40美元的低端產品。

B： 我們完全理解必須生產低成本產品的原因。不過，我想提出我的顧慮，我們如果我們不提高處理器的速度內置記憶體的大小，我們有風險恐怕不符合 **Android** 的要求。用戶在使用大部分的市售應用軟體時，將會有問題。

A： 你點出的問題沒錯。讓我們再看過所有的細節，並重新進行評估。

科技關鍵知識用語

1.portfolio　🄝　組合（產品組合，投資組合）

一種資訊內容的收集組合。用於金融投資，則是投資的分配組合。用於個人的工作生涯則是有關個人教育背景、工作資歷和技能的資訊組合。用於產品則是不同產品特性的組合。

This is the portfolio of this candidate.

這是該候選人的資料。

2.budget　🄝　預算

　　　　　🄐🄳🄹　經濟的，廉價的

We have concerned about the safety of those budget airlines.

我們對這些廉價航空公司的安全問題有顧慮。

133

3. raise Ⅴ 提出，舉起

Please raise your hand when your name is called.

當叫到你名字時請舉手。

4. compatible adv 相容的

They are compatible in all aspects and that is why they have a happy marriage.

他們在各方面都很相配，這就是為什麼他們有個快樂的婚姻。

5. aftermarket n 售後市場

You can download all the compatible applications in the aftermarket.

您可以在售後市場下載所有相容的應用程序。

6. assessment n 評估

We think John's assessment of the situation was spot-on.

我們認為約翰對這形勢判斷得很正確。

★ spot-on：完全正確

 句型解析

"run the risk of"中文解釋為「這樣做可能帶來……的風險、冒著……的危險」，對欲採取的行動判斷可能帶來的風險。也可以說是"at the risk of"，唯一不同的是這是一個介詞片語，而"run the risk of"是動詞片語。在使用的時候需依句中是否已出現動詞來做選擇。例如對話中的句子可改寫成：

We are <u>at the risk of</u> not being able to meet Android compatibility requirements.

句型延伸及範例

1. My doctor told me I'm running the risk of getting cardiovascular disease if I don't start doing exercise.

   我的醫生告訴我，如果我不開始做運動，我會有得到心血管疾病的風險。

2. We run the risk of being late for the product launch if you still can't decide which designing house to work with.

   如果你還不能決定哪家設計廠商，我們有無法按照產品上市計劃時程的風險。

3. I refused to run the risk of being dismissed.

   我拒絕冒可能會被開除的風險。

MEMO

As Per...

根據……

 **Dialogue**

A: Hi. I am calling to follow up on the shipment arrangements. We were supposed to receive the shipment two days ago. But until now, we've received no information about the ETA.

B: I think I can help. May I have your shipment number?

A: Yes, it is EVA2014012033.

B: OK, here it is. The shipment won't arrive for another week.

A: There must be something wrong. We ordered express delivery. Our need is urgent.

B: Sorry, ma'am. I just checked our system. **As per** your request, the order was made for regular speed shipment. If you like, we can send you a copy of the order, on which you will find signatures of your company's authorized personnel.

 對話譯文

A：你好，我打電話來問問看我們訂的貨應該在兩天前就該收到，但到目前為止，沒有收到預定抵達的日期。

B：讓我來幫您，請問您有貨運號碼嗎？

A：有，是 EVA2014012033。

B：找到了。一星期後才會抵達。

A：一定是搞錯了，我們特別要求要快遞運送，我們急著要這批貨。

B：不好意思，小姐。我剛才查了我們的系統，根據您的要求，這批貨是以普通速度運送。如果您要的話，我可以傳送訂單副本給您，上面有貴公司授權人員的簽字。

 科技關鍵知識用語

1. **ETA=estimated time of arrival**　預計抵達時間
   而另外 **ETD=estimated time of departure** 預計離開時間
   常見於船班和航班的時間表説法。

137

2.authorized personnel 被授權人員

The central control room is for authorized personnel only.

中控室僅准許被授權的人員進入。

3.the order was made 下訂單

這裡要強調下訂單的動詞是make。

Let me make the order.

讓我來下這訂單。

科技業無往不利的英語力

 句型解析

在一般日常對話中很少有人會用 **as per**，但在商業上常會用到。As per= In accordance with 翻譯為「根據……」，相關用法如下：

- as per advice　根據建議
- as per the attached list 根據附件
- as per company policy　根據公司策略
- as per our conversation　根據我們的對話
- as per your request　根據你的要求
- as per usual = as usual 根據過去情況

 句型延伸及範例

1.As per the attached list, you are not invited to the conference.

依照這名單，你並沒有被邀請參加會議。

2. As per our company policy, the annual leave of the current year is pro-rated when you resign.

根據公司的政策，當你辭職時，當年的年休假是按比例算。

3. As per our conversation, we both will throw in half million dollars to this project.

根據我們的談話，我們各將投入 50 萬美元在這案子上。

4. As per your request, we will combine the two payments into one.

根據您的要求，我們將把這兩筆款項合併為一。

See Where I'm Coming From?

你知道我在說什麼嗎？

Dialogue

科技業無往不利的英語力

A: A mobile phone is very personal, always on and always connected to the Internet. There is no user who doesn't want to customize his or her mobile phone by downloading aftermarket applications to extend functionality.

Without going into all the details, that's why we feel it is critical to design a product that is compatible with all Android requirements. Do you see where I am coming from?

B: Thanks for giving me the highlights. I do see your points. However, it is not that we didn't want to. We just experienced difficulties in delivering the results you expect.

 對話譯文

A：手機是非常個人化的，並且是 24 小時與物聯網連接。沒有一個人不想透過下載應用程序來客製化自己的手機，增加它的功能。不用再詳細說明，這就是為什麼設計出一個可靠的產品，並與 Android 完全相容是非常重要的。你知道我在說什麼嗎？

B：謝謝你特別地指出來，我了解你的看法。但是，並不是我們不想，而是我們有很大的困難來達到你所期望的結果。

 科技關鍵知識用語

1.**without go into all the details**　不進一步檢視細節
Without going into the details, his proposal was rejected.
沒經過進一步地檢視細節，他的企畫書就被否決了。

2.**highlight**　突出，強調，重點
Her speech is definitely the highlight of the night.
她的演說肯定是今晚的重點。

3. I see your points　我了解你的觀點

I see your point, but I'm afraid that I cannot agree with you.

我了解你的觀點，但我恐怕無法認同你的意見。

 句型解析

"See where I'm coming from?"「你知道我為什麼如此說嗎？」，在工作場所對話中很常用的說法，當做了很多解釋之後，覺得不須再多談一些細節，對方應該可以了解時，會說 "See where I'm coming from?"。

另外的說法："Do you understand the reasons why I'm saying this?"「你了解我這麼說的原因嗎？」，"Are you with me?"「你懂我的意思嗎？」都可替換使用。

而當不懂對方在說什麼的時候，則可以說 "Sorry, I'm not following." 或是 "Sorry, I didn't get it." 等來回應。

句型延伸及範例

1. I think I know what you mean. I know where you're coming from.

   我想我明白你的意思，我知道你在説什麼。

2. I have reminded you many times. Do you understand the reason why I am saying this?

   我已經提醒你很多次了，你明白我為什麼這樣説的原因嗎？

3. I have made my points clear. Are you with me?

   我已經説得很清楚了，你懂了嗎？

No Doubt About That!

毫無疑問

 **Dialogue**

科技業無往不利的英語力

A: How is the new project leader? I understand he just joined your team last month.

B: He is very professional and creative. As a result of his experience in this industry, he has an excellent personal network and good outside sources. It speeds our process and boosts morale. I think we will have no problem keeping to the schedule.

A: Oh, I have **no doubt about that**. I know he has been very good in the past with managing project schedules. He is very detail-oriented and executes well.

 對話譯文

A： 你們團隊的新專案經理表現得如何？我知道他上個月才剛剛加入。

B： 他是非常專業，非常有創造力。由於他在這個行業的經驗，他有很好的關係和人脈，這加快了整個案子的進度，也提振了士氣。我認為我們沒有任何問題可以準時完成這案子。

A： 我毫無疑問！我知道他對進度的掌握一直非常好，非常注重細節，執行力很強。

 科技關鍵知識用語

1. **speed up** 加速
The new system will definitely speed up the process.
這套新系統使整個程序增快不少。

2. **boost up** 提高、增強、提振
What he just said really boosted me up.
他剛才所說的讓我振奮不少。

145

也可以說成

What he just said really gave me a boost.

3. morale 　n　 士氣

After the loss, their morale went very low.

失敗之後,他們士氣很低落。

4. detail-oriented 　adj　 注重細節

We are looking for someone who is very detail-oriented.

我們在找的人必須非常注重細節。

 句型解析

"No doubt about that!"、"I have no doubt about that!"、"There is no doubt about that!"都是相同的意思,通常在句子一開始或是結束時使用,來強調對事情的信心和確定性。

doubt 是懷疑,不確定,無法決定的意思。跟 doubt 有關的其他用法還有:

★ beyond doubt—毋庸置疑

★ without a doubt/doubtless—毫無疑問

★ in doubt—懷疑

科技業無往不利的英語力

句型延伸及範例

1. No doubt about that! She will be elected, given those poll numbers.

   毫無疑問地，根據民意調查的結果，她一定會選上。

2. His appointment to this job is still in doubt.

   他這一個職務的任職與否尚在不明階段。

3. His integrity is beyond doubt.

   他的誠信是毋庸置疑的。

WEEK 5

No Doubt About That!

Let's Say...

比方說……

Dialogue

A: Hi, Jack. I was just about to go to your office.

B: What about, Simon?

A: Something wrong with our mock-up sample. We will need to go to the factory to have a look.

B: My experiences with that factory have been unpleasant. Can you bring me up to speed? What's going on this time?

A: I am rushing out. Let me go over the situation when we meet. **Let's say** we meet at 3:00 pm in the foyer. I will drive.

B: Great. See you then!

 對話譯文

A：嗨，Jack，我正要去你的辦公室。

B：什麼事，Simon？

A：我們的實體樣品在工廠製作時碰到問題，我們必須去工廠看看。

B：我與這家工廠的合作經驗一直不是很愉快。告訴我，這次是怎麼回事？

A：我正趕著要出去，等我們碰面後，我再把整個情況告訴你。比方說，我們下午 3 點在大廳碰面，我開車。

B：好，到時見！

 科技關鍵知識用語

1. rush out 趕著出去

Everyone rushes out when they smell the smoke.

當他們聞到煙味的時候，每個人都衝了出去。

科技業無往不利的英語力

2. bring me up to speed　告訴我最新消息（最新情況）

After the competitive bidding, do remember to phone me and bring me up to the speed.

在競標結束之後，請一定要記得打電話給我，告訴我最新的消息。

3. go over　檢視

Let's go over the evidence carefully.

讓我們仔細檢視這些證據。

4. foyer　n　大廳，大樓入口處，玄關

Let's meet in the foyer of this building after the meeting.

開完會後，我們就在大樓的入口碰面。

 句型解析

"let's say" 是在對話中常常聽到，非正式口語化的說法，可放在句子的任何位置，通常前後會接逗點，有「例如」、「大約」、「比方說」的意思，所以在正式的場合或演說當中通常不會用 "let's say"，但在日常對話或 email 溝通上則非常好用也常聽到，用來說明一個建議或可能發生的情況。

1. I don't really remember the time, but we went home right after the game. Let's say, we got home at 11pm.

   我實在不記得時間，但我們比賽之後就回家了，大概是晚上 11 點到家的。

2. Try to finish the work by, let's say, Friday.

   試著完成這個工作，讓我們說週五以前。

3. Let's say the journey takes two hours. You'll arrive here at two o'clock.

   比方說這車程大約兩個小時，你會在兩點鐘到達這裡。

4. It takes about, let's say, three kilos of beef to prepare this meal.

   大約需要，比方說要用到三公斤牛肉來準備這一頓飯。

In the First Place...

一開始的時候……

A: Based on the numbers I received from you dated January 15, I have finished the first draft of the 3D layout drawing. Knowing how urgently you need the drawing for the meeting today, I made the project top priority. It still took me a whole week to complete. Please have a look. Your feedback is appreciated.

B: Thank you so much for all the effort! Actually, this customer has postponed the meeting. They say they gave us an incomplete set of data. They will schedule another meeting after a run of data collecting and updating our numbers.

A: This is news to me. I wish you had told me **in the first place** that you were having these issues. I delayed other projects to bring this one forward.

 對話譯文

A：根據一月十五日收到你提供的數據，我已經完成 **3D** 立體配置圖的初稿，知道你緊急在今天會議中需要這圖，我把它列為首要工作項目，花了我整整一個禮拜的時間才完成。請看看，歡迎任何意見。

B：非常感謝你努力完成它。事實上，客戶已延後這案子，因他們給我們的數據不是完整的，等他們收集好另一組新的數據後，會再另外安排會議。

A：怎麼我不知道，你應該在一開始時就告知我有關可能的情況。為了這案子，我將其他案子延後先做這案子。

 科技關鍵知識用語

1.dated adj 過期的；註有日期的

I am writing this email to confirm the receipt of your letter dated 2015-01-21.

我寫這封郵件來確認收到你 2015 年 1 月 21 日送出的信件。

She used rather dated data for the design.

她用相當陳舊的數據來進行設計。

2. know　Ⅴ　知道

Knowing you would be hungry, I brought a sandwich.

知道你會餓，所以我帶了一個三明治。

3. postpone　Ⅴ　延後

The business trip has been postponed for some time.

這次出差已延了一段時間。

4. bring forward　提前

I would like to bring forward the quarterly review. Let's do it next week rather than wait.

我想把季檢討提前，不要等了，下星期就做。

句型解析

"in the first place" 常使用的說法，有「一開始的時候」的意思，很好用的短短幾個字，可將句子的語氣很正確的表達。

另外的解釋，則可做「在幾個不同重要程度中排列第一位的事項」的意思。

句型延伸及範例

1. Why didn't you tell me in the first place that you had decided to leave?

你為什麼不一開始就告訴我，你已經決定離開？

2. He could have bought a new one in the first place.

他一開始就該買個新的。

3. You shouldn't have taken the job in the first place.

你本來就不應該接受這份工作。

4. I am not joining the club because, in the first place, its shower room didn't look clean.

我沒有加入那俱樂部，最重要的是因為淋浴間不是很乾淨。

MEMO

An Opportunity Presents Itself...

當機會來臨時……

Dialogue

A: Hey, Jerry. How have you been? Glad to see you again. This exhibition is always a good place for the reunion party, isn't it? We see each other once every year in the exhibition. How long have we known each other?

B: I think it has been ten years. Yeah, I remember when we met, you were an entry-level staff engineer. Look at you now: a senior manager leading a team of 12. You are really making headway. Really stepping up.

A: Well, thanks. But your job is every bit as challenging as mine. No doubt you've been promoted as well.

B: Actually, I haven't. I still work on the design team and hold the same title I always have. When <u>an opportunity presents itself</u>, though, I plan to ask our division chief for a promotion. I'm eyeing the team leader's role, which has just opened up.

對話譯文

A：嘿，Jerry，你最近好嗎？很高興又看到你，這展覽像個同學會，大家都在這碰面，不是嗎？在這展覽我們每年見面一次，而我們認識多久了？

B：我覺得應該有十年。當我們認識時，你只是一名新手工程師。現在看你，一個領 12 人團隊的高級經理。你正步步高升。

A：哈！謝謝。你的工作不比我的簡單，毫無疑問你也升官了吧？

B：其實沒有。仍然在設計組掛一樣的頭銜。然而一有機會時，我想跟我部門主管談一下升遷的機會，我的目標是現在空出來的設計組負責人的位置。

 科技關鍵知識用語

1.entry-level job　低階工作

Given his experience, he is over qualified for an entry-level job.

以他的工作經驗，低階工作不適合他。

157

2. **make headway**　有進展中

We are making headway to finish the project.

我們目前完成這個案子的進展相當順利。

3. **open up**　打開；開放（用於工作時，則是剛釋出在找人的工作）

I have seen many jobs open up in Google lately.

我看到谷歌最近有許多的工作空缺在找人。

 句型解析

"**present itself**"有出現、發生、升起的意思。"**an opportunity present itself**" 則解釋為「一有機會的時候」。

例如

The teacher will educate the students whenever the opportunity presents itself.

這老師一有機會就會教導學生。

另外 "**present oneself**" 有到達、出現、參與

例如

She presented herself in John's funeral.

她出現在John的喪禮中。

科技業無往不利的英語力

句型延伸及範例

1. When opportunity presents itself, take it.

   當機會一出現，把握住它。

2. Maria and Jennifer say if opportunity presents itself, they would love to sing together.

   Maria和Jennifer說，如果有機會她們願意一起唱歌。

3. Once an opportunity presents itself, I won't let it slip away.

   一旦機會出現，我不會讓它溜走。

Refresh Someone's Memory

提醒某人

 Dialogue

A: Thanks for the presentation. We are very keen to proceed with the agreement, but we have questions about one point: pricing. It appears your prices have been hiked since our last discussion.

B: Mr. Kim, as a matter of fact, the price structure is the same as in our last quote. The scenarios are different. Let me **refresh your memory**: the prices in our last proposal are quoted based on bulk pack in volume. The prices shown here are for commercial packaging with the same volume criteria. Depending on your requirement, both of these options are doable.

科技業無往不利的英語力

 對話譯文

A：謝謝你的簡報，我們很希望能進行簽約，但只有一個問題：價格。在我看來，你把價格拉高了。

B：金先生，事實上，價格結構是與上次報價是一樣的，只是不同的情況。讓我回顧一下：在上次提出的價格是根據工業包裝的大量價格。

以相同的量標準，這個報價是商業包裝。依據您的需求，這兩種選擇都是可行的。

 科技關鍵知識用語

1.**as a matter of fact** 事實上 (= in fact; actually)

She pretends to understand, but as a matter of fact, she doesn't.

她裝作懂，事實上並不懂。

2.**scenario** n 方案；腳本

A possible scenario would be that we bring in the 2nd source of parts and do running change in the production line.

一種可能的情況是，我們引進零件的第二供貨來源在生產線上進行改變。

The best-case scenario would be for us to complete the field try by tomorrow.

在最好的情況下將是我們明天完成實測。

In the worst-case scenario, we would have to start the

production all over again.

在最壞的情況下，我們將不得不重新生產。

3. **appear**　Ⅴ　出現

很平常的用法: he appears. 他出現了。

但當用於問題或狀況時，則有浮現的意味（問題已存在）

The problem appears when you drive the car after 10 minutes.

當車開十分鐘後，問題就會發生（浮現）。

  句型解析

"**refresh someone's memory**"意思是提醒某人一些過去已知道/被告知的事，藉由提供一些資訊或回顧事情經過來提醒人。

"**refresh**" 也有重新注入活力之意，如當有國外來的訪客，下機後，可詢問是否要先到飯店梳洗一下再進公司。

例如

Would you like to refresh a bit in your hotel before we go into office?

您是否要先到飯店梳洗一下之後，再進公司呢？

（在這裡 'refresh'也可換說成 'freshen up'或 'freshen yourself'）

"**refreshing**"，形容詞，有清涼令人振奮的解釋。

On a hot summer day, there's nothing more refreshing than

WEEK 6

科技業無往不利的英語力

a cold beer.

在炎熱的夏天，沒有什麼比一杯冰冷啤酒更讓人沁心涼。

"refreshment"則是清涼飲料和小點。在國外一些觀光景點，可看到"Refreshment"的牌子，是販賣咖啡、飲料、小點之處。

 句型延伸及範例

1. I couldn't remember what that old man was called. Judy had to refresh my memory.

   我不記得那老人叫什麼，Judy不得不提醒我的記憶。

2. Can you refresh my memory as to how to fill out this landing form?

   你能提醒我一下如何填寫這張入境表格。

3. I slept in the office last night. Let me refresh before we start the discussion.

   我昨晚睡在辦公室裡，讓我梳洗一下再開始我們的討論。

Bring to Someone's Attention

引起某人的注意

 **Dialogue**

A: Hi, everyone. I have listed the feedback comments from power users and out-of-box reviews in the leading tech blogs. This list prioritizes the issues that remain on this new product and gives us areas to improve.

B: No doubt this is very useful information. But a colleague has already **brought** point four—battery strength—**to my attention**.

It's going to be very unsatisfying for our customers to find their batteries out of juice after just half a day of use.

A mobile phone is a very personal item now and you won't go out the door without taking it with you. I strongly recommend that we make a top priority of addressing this.

 **對話譯文**

A： 嗨，大家好。我在這裡列出一些超級手機用戶使用後的回饋意見和一些科技部落客所寫的開箱評論。我將他們對這款新產品的問題回饋整

理出優先順序，這是我們需要加強改進的地方。

B： 毫無疑問的這些都是非常有用的資訊。但有人指出第四點有關電池續航力特別引起我的注意。如果電池在半天內就消耗殆盡，這對用戶來說無法令人滿意。手機是一個很私人的隨身物品，你出門一定會帶著它。我強烈建議要仔細進一步瞭解這問題。

 ## 科技關鍵知識用語

1. out-of-box review　　開箱文

現在網路上很常見的文章，尤其是科技產品，從打開箱子瞬間的帶給人的感受跟使用後的用戶親身體驗的文章。尤其對科技用戶，許多科技網站的開箱文具有相當大的購買影響力。

The out-of-box reviews in all the tech blogs highlight for their readers many of the same concerns about purchasing our product.

所有的科技部落格的開箱文中，對讀者提出在購買我們的產品之前都有相同的顧慮。

2. prioritize　ⓥ　把……區分優先次序；排序

How do you prioritize your work?

你是如何安排你的工作的優先順序？

3. areas to improve 改善部分、方向

在工作場所很好用的說法，可以是每個員工的自我評量需改善的部分，可以是產品需改善的部分，或是組織團隊需改善的部分

Please put down three areas to improve in your personal appraisal.

請在你的個人評量中請列出三項須改善的部分。

4. no doubt 不容置疑

I have no doubt about his loyalty.

我對他的忠誠度不容置疑。

5. run out of juice 電池快沒了

juice 中文為果汁，但一般俗用時可做電池電量的說法。
另外也可用 flat 這個字來形容快沒電了。

My battery is pretty flat.

我的電池量很低了。

其他對電池電量的描述還有:
Battery is exhausted (or dead).

電池沒電了。

 句型解析

"bring to someone's attention"用於當你在一段對話中或資訊交流

中，某些過去曾有的對話或資訊引起你的關注，而你也希望其他人能有相同看法和關注。

 句型延伸及範例

1. The riot last night has brought to the government's attention about the social benefit for low income group.
昨晚的暴動讓政府重視到有關低收戶的社會福利。

2. What you have just said has brought to my attention about how unhappy you are with your job.
你所說的話讓我注意到你對工作的不滿意。

For That Matter

就此而言

 **Dialogue**

A: I can't agree with your proposal to appoint only one client in the Australian market. In view of market size, Australia promises far more opportunities for us than a single client can provide. We would be tying our hands.

B: I can't agree with you more, **for that matter**, if we have a full range of products available for this market. The catch is that we are not doing that.

On the contrary: Australia has special requirements that affect the specifications, and right now we only have two products that meet the requirements. But the following year will offer us a chance to review the channel landscaping which we have more products available.

科技業無往不利的英語力

 對話譯文

A：我不同意你的看法在澳洲市場只委任一個客戶。看看它的市場規模，絕對需要多於一個客戶，你會讓自己綁手綁腳。

B：就此而言，如果在我們擁有完整產品線的情況下，我再同意你不過，但情形並非這樣。

而且剛好相反，我們只有兩個產品符合澳洲特殊產品規格的要求。不過一年後，我們能有更多的產品，到時就可重新評估銷售通路的規劃。

 科技關鍵知識用語

1. **appoint** Ⅴ 指定。另外也常用 assign。

He has appointed me as his successor.

他指定我為他的接班人。

2. **tie someone's hands/get someone's hands tied** 綁手綁腳

You have got your hands tied by letting your members to help with other projects.

你讓自己團隊的人去協助其他案子這讓你自己綁手綁腳。

169

3. full range of products　整個產品線

用來形容產品線的説法 例如 product range，另外也可用 product portfolio。

Their product portfolio is very impressive.

他們的產品組合讓人驚豔。

4. channel landscape　通路分布狀況

landscape 解釋為景觀，山水。在商業上可用來描述分布狀況。

His company coming into this industry will change the whole landscape for product supply.

他的公司進入這個產業，讓整個產品供貨分布情況完全改變。

 句型解析

"for that matter"「就此而言」、「説到那一點」、「至於那件事」，此説法帶出你對某件事情的關心，進一步加以強化。另外説法 "So far as that is concerned" 和 "Concerning that..."。

科技業無往不利的英語力

句型延伸及範例

1. My days have been hectic, unable to squeeze in any more meetings. For that matter, I can assign the most capable one of my subordinates to attend the meeting.

   我的行程非常忙碌，無法再插入任何會議。對於這個問題，我可以指派我手下最有能力的人參加這個會議。

2. My doctor has strongly suggested that I should rest more. For that matter, I would like to cut down the time at work.

   我的醫生強烈建議我多休息。關於這個問題，我想減少工作的時間。

MEMO

Your Point Is Taken

 **Dialogue**

科技業無往不利的英語力

A: Model M9 has been out in the market for five months. The original product roadmap was to bring in a new model to replace M9 after four more months. The good news is that we are making headway in meeting this schedule. But we have some choices to make. The new Android OS upgrade is due for release in five months. That's earlier than we expected. In this case, it would mean we launch a new product one month before the new OS is released. That would leave us in an awkward situation, as our product will look outdated soon after launch. Therefore, we might want to continue selling M9 till we have the new OS integrated with our new product. That would mean delaying the release of Model M10 another six or seven months.

B: From my point of view, it seems we risk losing market share if we drag M9 all that way when so many competitors are pushing newer products. I think we should offer an intermediate upgrade to M9 at that four-month mark. We can boost its camera performance and sound quality, offer more color selections for the case, or add any other features that anyone here can think of. That allows M9 to continue for a few more months while creating some fresh buzz, as we prepare to launch M10 as quickly as we can.

A: **Your point is well taken**. It's an appealing option from a marketing standpoint, but we will need to examine the cost-effectiveness of doing that.

對話譯文

A: 我們的產品 M9 已經在市場上持續銷售 5 個月。原來的產品計畫是在四個月後有新的產品取代 M9。好消息是我們照時間表進展順利，但我們有一些選擇要做， 五個月後新版本的 Android OS 會出來，比我們預期的早。在這種情況下，我們面對推出新產品一下變成過時產品的尷尬局面。因此，我們可能不得不繼續銷售 M9 直到新的操作系統準備好，也就是 M10 要等 6-7 個月後才能推出。

B: 從我的角度來看，當這麼多競爭對手的新產品都陸續出來，而我們用 M9 的拖延戰術會讓我們失去市場占有率。我認為我們可以四個月後推出 M9 進階機種，藉由改善 M9 的相機的性能，音質和提供更多的顏色選擇，或其他任何人能想到的任何其他功能，來度過那幾個月，直到我們推出全新機種 M10。

A：我絕對接受你的觀點，以行銷角度來看是不錯的選擇，但讓我們再研究一下它的經濟效益。

 科技關鍵知識用語

1.roadmap n 路線圖

科技業常用到 **product roadmap** 來呈現組織短期和長期的產品目標，依據科技演進的產品與程序方案來制定出的產品計畫表。

2.awkward adj 為難的，麻煩的，不合宜的

It would put him in a very awkward position.

這會使他處境非常尷尬。

3.drag v 拖，拖動，拖著（腳、尾巴等）；硬拖（某人）做（某事）或至（某地）

Though she felt exhausted after a long day at work, she dragged herself off to the night class.

雖然在漫長的一天工作後感到疲憊，她仍拖著疲憊身軀去上夜校。

The meeting always drags when we get to the R&D report.

這會議一旦講到研發報告就會拖很久。

 句型解析

"**point is taken**"、"**someone's point is well taken**" 表示某人的看法和意見被接受，且被認同，在工作上是很好的用法。而更簡短的說法

"point taken" 可以代表相同意思。

"point" 在這裡代表某人觀點和看法。另外跟 "point" 有關的常用説法：
"Have I made my points clear?"「我有把我的看法説清楚了嗎？」，也就是説「你了解我的看法了嘛？」

 句型延伸及範例

1. Your point is well-taken and it will not be forgotten.
很認同你的看法，也不會忘記這一點的。

2. Your point is taken and no need to say more. Let's move on to the next.
很同意你的看法，不需再多説了，讓我們看下一個。
（這種説法有點不禮貌，也可能是發表意見的人停不下來，才會有這樣的對話。）

3. Have I made my points clear? Do you need more elaboration?
我有把我的想法説清楚了嗎？你需要更多的闡述嗎？

Hardly vs. Barely

幾乎不 **vs.** 勉強可以

 **Dialogue**

科技業無往不利的英語力

A: Gosh, I <u>barely</u> understand his English through the whole speech. His Russian accent is so strong that is so difficult for a non-English speaker to catch his words. Fortunately, I know the technology he was talking about and caught the jargon. Listening for the terminology helped me follow him. Such great ideas! He's really opening up the doors to the future world. Impressive!

B: The topic of the speech was completely new to me. I <u>hardly</u> understood any of it. I'm glad I got a copy of the handouts for study.

WEEK 7

Hardly vs. Barely

 對話譯文

A：天哪，整個演講我勉強可以聽懂他的英文，他的俄羅斯口音真重，對英文非母語的人還真難聽得懂，還好我很清楚演講所涉及的技術內容及行話。由這一些關鍵技術用語，我還能聽懂他所説的內容。他的演講有如開了一扇門，讓我看到未來的世界。太令人印象深刻！

B：在演講的題目對我是全新的東西，我幾乎聽不懂任何東西。還好有講義讓我研究一下。

 科技關鍵知識用語

1.**accent** ⓝ 口音

His has a very German accent.

他的德國口音非常重。

2.**jargon** ⓝ 專業語言、行話

He used a lot of police jargon in his criminal novel.

他在他的犯罪小説中用了很多警察的行話。

3.**terminology** ⓝ 術語、專用名詞

He knows a lot of terminology about bio-tech, especially

human cloning.

他知道很多有關生物科技的專用名詞，尤其是有關人類複製方面的。

4. handouts　n　講義

Please pass out the handouts.

請將講義發下去。

The handouts for the presentation are on the table at the door. Please take one.

簡報的講義放在門旁的桌上，請拿一份。

句型解析

"hardly" －幾乎不，簡直不，僅僅

"barely" －勉強可以。

兩者說法幾乎可互相取代，但在表達程度上仍有些小差別。"hardly" 通常是幾乎沒做到，而 "barely" 則有差點做不到。舉個簡單例子：

Because of the traffic, we hardly made it to the party on time.

由於交通擁擠，我們幾乎沒法準時參加聚會。（可能結果遲到30秒）

Because of the traffic, we barely made it to the party on time.

由於交通擁擠，我們差點沒法準時參加聚會。（可能結果為只早到了30秒）

在這兩種說法之間可能到達聚會時僅僅一、兩分鐘差別，但在心情的描述上不須精確的時間要求時，兩者的使用可以相同。

句型延伸及範例

1. You proposal hardly meets the requirements.
   你的提議沒有達到需求。

2. He was hardly aware that it was happening.
   他幾乎沒有覺察到事情發生了。

3 Their performance is barely satisfactory.
   他們的表演尚差強人意。

4 My income barely covers my expenses.
   我的收入剛剛夠用。

5 My income hardly covers my expense.
   我的收入不夠用。

Give Yourself Credit (for...)

給自己一些肯定／要對自己有信心

 **Dialogue**

科技業無往不利的英語力

A: My boss reviewed our exhibit and apparently didn't find it satisfactory. Our booth had fewer visitors than expected. She says our design didn't stand out and didn't reflect clearly the nature of our core business.

She also wants to see us using more clever ideas for DM. Sounds like I made a hash of things.

B: I think you should <u>give yourself more credit</u>. Considering you filled in for someone on short notice and never did this before, you did an outstanding job.

Running the booth at a trade show is demanding work. Give yourself credit for doing a difficult job well.

 對話譯文

A：剛剛我的老闆跟我檢討這次秀展的結果，顯然她不是那麼滿意。她認為訪客數比預期少，我們的攤位設計並不夠顯眼，呈現的訊息沒有傳達我們的核心業務本質。

她希望 DM 能更清楚地傳達意念。聽起來我搞砸了。

B：我覺得你應該給自己更多功勞，要有信心。看看你短時間被要求接手別人的工作來準備你未曾做過的展覽準備。

展場攤位的管理是一個相當繁瑣的工作，能完成這困難的工作，你該給自己更多的肯定。

 科技關鍵知識用語

1. stand out Ⅴ phr 脫穎而出
outstanding adj 傑出的
Since the first day in school, she stands out from her classmates.
自從學校第一天，她就從同學中脫穎而出。

181

2. running the booth　維持、管理展場的攤位

His colleagues were not up to running the booth without him.

如果沒有他，他的同事們是無法管理好這個展場的攤位。

3. make a hash of　搞砸

The newly elected city mayor made a hash of his first public speech.

新選出的市長把他的第一場公開演講搞砸了。

 句型解析

"**give yourself credit for**" 意思是你已盡力，縱使結果不如預期，也不否定一切的努力付出和結果，這是在工作場所中很常見的情況，所以解釋為「要給自己點功勞和認可，要對自己有信心」、告訴自己「你做的比自己想像的還好」、「你做的沒那麼糟」。

科技業無往不利的英語力

句型延伸及範例

1. You have made it this far, please give yourself credit for doing it. Don't give up!

   妳已堅持到現在，妳做的沒那麼糟，給自己點肯定，不要放棄！

2. Being a single parent is not an easy job. Look at your children. They are doing well in school. Give yourself credit for it.

   作為一個單親媽媽並不容易，看看妳的孩子，在學校都很優秀，要給自己點信心，妳做得很好。

MEMO

By the Same Token

同樣理由

 **Dialogue**

Cathy: Hi, Melissa. You didn't attend the meeting yesterday. How's everything? I heard you were not feeling well.

Melissa: I am fine, Cathy. I took yesterday off. To be honest, I was really having a job interview with the biggest player in the market. I got a job offer!

Cathy: Wow, sounds great. How come you don't look more excited? I'd be flying.

Melissa: I am struggling over the decision, actually. When you work in a big multi-national company, the income is better and the employee benefits are good, but **by the same token**, you are a small potato. In my job here I have authority to make decisions and my boss appreciates my creativity. I'm concerned that over there I might be just a follower.

 對話譯文

Cathy：嗨，**Melissa**。妳昨天沒參加會議，怎麼了？聽説妳不舒服。

Melissa：我很好，**Cathy**。我昨天請假。説實話，我去了市場最大咖那裡面試，而且我錄取了。

Cathy：哇，聽起來很不錯。但為什麼妳看起來不是很興奮，要我已經高興地飛上天了。

Melissa：其實我對於決定是否接受那工作感到很掙扎。在一個大的跨國公司工作，收入和員工福利都較好，但因為同樣理由，在那裡只是個小螺絲釘。我在這裡的工作有做決定的權力，我的老闆欣賞我的創意。而在那家公司，我可能只是個聽令者。

 科技關鍵知識用語

1. **take off**　"take off" 的用法有非常多，根據使用的方式有不同的意思，下面是工作上比較常看到的説法：

a.　休假，請假

I am going to take a few days off.

我將休假幾天。

b. 起飛

The plane is timed to take off at 8 am.

飛機定於上午八點起飛。

When the economy took off, the GDP grew to USD$8000.

當經濟起飛時,人均國內生產毛額成長到八千美元。

c. 脫掉

He took off the shirt.

他脫去了上衣。

d. 離開,動身前往

My boss called me to his office before he took off for his business trip.

老闆在他動身出差前叫我去他辦公室。

e. 匆匆離開

She took off for the school at a run.

她匆忙離開向學校跑去。

f. 開始流行;突然走紅

When Apple launched its iPhone, the smartphone sales started to take off.

當蘋果推出 iPhone,智慧型手機的銷售開始盛行。

3. **small potato**　　小囉囉;小螺絲釘

小心!在英文上不是用 small screw 來形容小螺絲釘角色

I am just a small potato in this company.

在這公司我只是個小螺絲釘。

句型解析

"token" 通常解釋為代幣（譬如遊樂場代幣），雖然代幣兩面印有不同圖樣，不論哪一面都是代幣，有如「事情的一體兩面」。而 **"by the same token"**，就解釋為「出於同樣的原因；同樣理由」。

 句型延伸及範例

1. Martin: I really feel cheated!
   Daisy: You think Bob cheated you, but, by the same token, he believes that you cheated him.
   Martin：我真的感覺被騙了！
   Daisy：你覺得鮑勃欺騙你，但同樣的理由，他認為你欺騙了他。

2. Her office colleagues tell me she is really a sweetheart, but by the same token others are put off by her manner.
   她的同事說她真是個甜姐兒，但因同樣理由，其他人對她的態度很反感。

3. The Captain demands total loyalty from his crews, but by the same token he offers the loyalty in return.
   船長要求所有水手對他完全忠誠可靠，基於同樣的原因，他對所有下屬也忠誠可靠。

My Take on...

Dialogue

科技業無往不利的英語力

A: We have received a long email from the customer with lots of complaints. The pricing, the delivery time, the term of payment, the quality of after-sales service, etc. They just acknowledged receipt of the first shipment yesterday and today we got the email. After checking with the production center, we found that two more shipments will be ready in a week. The customer has put us in the difficult position of holding all production work for now or just shipping out the goods as we originally agreed.

B: Hold on. Let me read the email.
Well, <u>my take on</u> it is that they are seeking reasons for a price reduction. We will have to be careful in crafting a reply. I'm not sure how best to handle that yet, but let me sleep on it.

 對話譯文

A： 我們收到客戶送來長長的電子郵件，有很多的抱怨，像是價格、交貨期、付款方式、以及售後服務的品質等。他們昨天才確認收到第一批貨，今天我們就收到這電子郵件。我剛與生產中心確認後，還有兩批貨一個星期內會出。現在我們有個難題是要停止所有的生產工作還是照原定出貨。

B： 等一下，讓我看看這電子郵件。
嗯，我對這電子郵件的看法，他們在找理由要求降價，我們要小心如何回答。讓我想想，明天再說，我現在還不知如何處理。

 科技關鍵知識用語

1. **receipt** 🔟 收據，收到

a. This is to acknowledge receipt of your letter.
來函已收到。

b. I've got receipt for the purchase.
我有這次採購的收據。

另外商用書信中的使用：

In receipt of your letter, we have made the payment accordingly.

收到妳的來信，我們依照要求付款。

2. **outgoing** adj 即將離開，即將離任，外向開朗

    a. We all offered glowing tributes to the outgoing CEO.

        我們都向即將卸任的執行長致敬。

    b. Her personality is very forceful and outgoing, completely different from her sister.

        她的個性非常堅強、開朗，跟她姐姐完全不一樣。

3. **sleep on it**　「有今晚想想，不用馬上回答」意思

You don't have to give me your decision now. Sleep on it, and let me know tomorrow.

妳不用現在決定，想一想，明天再告訴我。

 句型解析

"**take on**"有好些不同的用法，如下：

· 做「擔任，承擔」解釋

He takes on more jobs and responsibilities.

他承擔了更多的工作及責任。

· 做「對付，對抗其他競爭者」解釋

He took on all other opponents.

他對抗著其他所有的敵人。

科技業無往不利的英語力

· 做「雇用」解釋

The factory took on more workers during the peak season.
工廠在旺季時雇用更多的工人。

而 **"my take on"** 解釋為「我的看法」、「我的感覺」、「我的詮釋」，
只要把 **"take"** 換成 "opinion"，"impression"，或是 "interpretation"
則可很容易了解。

 ## 句型延伸及範例

1. My take on his responses is that he just wants to be alone.
   Let's give him some privacy.
   我對他回應的看法是，他想一個人靜靜。讓我們給他一些隱私。

2. My take on the regulation set out by the military is that
   they want to reduce the number of incidents involving
   enlisted men on leave.
   我對軍方採取的調控是要減少軍人休假外出時的任何事故發生。

3. My take on the new policy is that the government authority
   wants to discourage real estate speculation. It's about
   time!
   我對政府新政策的看法是，他們想阻止人們對房地產的投機心態。也是
   時候了！

Gets Under One's Skin

讓……感到不舒服

Dialogue

科技業無往不利的英語力

A: Ray is really a genius who thinks outside the box. Whenever we found ourselves in a dead end, he always came up with something to solve the problem.

For a nerd like him, his way of thinking is very bold and creative.

B: Indeed! I have to agree with you, from that perspective. But his approach to communication **gets under my skin**.

He invariably launches discussion with some statements intended to make other people feel stupid, then cites mind-numbing numbers and data before he gets down to the business.

 對話譯文

A：**Ray** 真的是天才，總是另類思考。當我們發現處在窮途末路時，他總能想出一些解決問題的辦法。像他這樣的書呆子，他的思維方式是非常大膽且有創意。

B：的確，從這個角度來看我同意你的看法。但他的溝通方式讓我很不舒服。他總是先說些話讓別人覺得自己很笨，接著舉出許多麻痺頭腦的數字和資料，最後才能進入主題。

🖥️ 科技關鍵知識用語

1. think outside the box 跳出框架思考，另類思考
Please don't limit yourself, think outside the box and explore any possibility.
請不要侷限自己，跳出框架思考和探索所有可能性。

2. dead end 死巷
It is a dead end. We're not going anywhere.
碰到死巷了，我們哪裡也去不得了（也可解釋成：我們沒有任何進展）。

科技業無往不利的英語力

3. **nerd** n 書呆子

nerdy adj 傻瓜似的

He is a computer nerd.

他是個電腦怪咖。

4. **bold** adj 大膽的，鹵莽的，冒失的，富有想像力的

This approach is definitely bold.

這舉動很大膽。

5. **cite** v 舉例，引用

I can cite quite a few instances to illustrate.

我可以舉出好幾件事來說明。

6. **mind-numbing** adj 令人頭腦麻木的

Presenting too many numbers can be mind-numbing for your audience.

太多的數字可以讓聽者頭腦麻木。

句型解析

"**gets under one's skin**"意味某人做的某些事，說的某些話或某種舉動讓某人覺得很不舒服，甚至激怒人。

另外也有完全相反的說法，但較不常用，就是對迷戀的人念念不忘。在 Cole Porter 的愛情歌曲中就用 "I've Got You Under My Skin" 來描述。

句型延伸及範例

1. When I hear people say women are bad drivers, it really gets under my skin.

當我聽到有人說女人都是很糟的駕駛時，真的讓我很生氣。

2. My brother likes to crack his knuckles. That really gets under my skin.

我弟弟喜歡折手指頭弄得嘎嘎響，那真讓我討厭。

3. Sure, she talks to everyone like we're three years old. But don't let her get under your skin.

我知道她跟每個人說話的樣子好像我們都是三歲小孩，但不要讓她影響到妳的心情。

MEMO

Keep One's Head Above Water

在困境裡掙扎

Dialogue

A: What's going on? You've got a cloud over your face.

B: Well, it happens that our new device hangs easily after it has been running for half an hour. I tried several different approaches to solve the problem but the device seems to have a mind of its own.

My own mind is blank. I have no idea now what to do.

A: The company has invested heavily in this project. If we release a lousy product, it's going to be tough for this organization to **keep its head above water**.

科技業無往不利的英語力

 對話譯文

A：怎麼了？你看起來滿臉烏雲密佈。

B：嗯，我們的新手機只要使用半小時後，就很容易當機。我已經嘗試了幾種不同的方法來解決問題，但機子好像不聽使喚。現在我的腦子裡一片空白，無計可施。

A：公司已投入很大資金在這案子上，如果我們上市一個糟糕的產品，公司將很難不陷入財務困境。

 科技關鍵知識用語

1. a cloud over someone's face 臉上一片烏雲

She got a cloud over her face after the customer turned down her proposal the third time.

在客戶第三次拒絕她的提議之後，她臉上一片烏雲。

2. mind goes blank 腦中一片空白

My mind went blank as the customer pointed out the mistakes in my presentation in front of the audience.

當客戶在所有聽眾面前指出我簡報中的錯誤時，我的腦子裡一片空白。

3. has its own mind 　有它自己的想法（或意識）

When I pressed the button, the robot was supposed to walk to the other side. Instead, it seemed to have its own mind. It walked to the opposite side to avoid a collision with the other robot.

當我按下按鈕，這個機器人應該走到另一邊。但是它好像有自己的想法一樣。它走向另一邊，以避免跟另一個機器人相撞。

 句型解析

"keep one's head above water"形容將溺水的人，努力把頭伸出水面，用來比喻拚了命做某些事，免於陷入困境（尤其是財務困境），或工作量太大，已無法呼吸。

句型延伸及範例

1. We have so many orders that we can hardly keep our heads above water.

   我們接了超多的訂單，以致於我們都快要忙死了。

2. It's all I can do to keep my head above water with the work I have. I can't take on any more.

   我能做的僅僅是在我所有的大量工作中求生存。我快要受不了。

3. The cost of living in Taipei is now so high that some might need to have two jobs just to keep their heads above water.

   台北的生活費現在是如此之高，有些人必須做兩份工作才得以維持生活。

MEMO

On the Grid

 **Dialogue**

科技業無往不利的英語力

A: What are you looking at? Big news? You can't take your eyes away from your phone.

B: I am updating my activities on a few different social networks. Just be patient with me for a few minutes. I will finish this soon.

(A while later…)

B: Okay, I'm done. Sorry to keep you waiting. Are you on any social networks? They can be very useful for marketing.

A: Not really, I am not a big fan of those. Simply put, I like to have my own privacy. I don't feel comfortable disclosing my schedule, daily activities, hobbies, and lifestyle choices to the geeks who run these sites.

B: I understand. But when you look at the evolution of recent technology, with cloud computing and wearable tech coming into our lives, you realize the applications are going to be enormous. When all is said and done, everyone will be "on the grid" even when they try not to be.

 對話譯文

A： 你在看什麼？有什麼大新聞嗎？你的眼睛好像離不開你的手機。

B： 我把我的活動更新到我的幾個不同網路社群頁面。再給我幾分鐘，我很快就好了。

（過了一會兒……）

B： 好了，抱歉讓你久等了。你有玩哪一種嗎？它們是很好的行銷工具。

A： 倒是沒有，我不是他們的粉絲。只是因為我喜歡有自己的隱私。把我所有的日常活動、行程、我的嗜好和興趣都提供給那些管理這些社群軟體程序的人，我覺得不舒服。

B： 我了解。但是，看看最近的技術演進，雲端和各式各樣的穿戴裝置進入我們的生活中，它們所產生的應用程式是無與倫比。不論如何，每個人都將會是「透過網路與世界連結」的，即使你不想。

 科技關鍵知識用語

1. sorry to keep you waiting 抱歉讓你久等了。

尤其用於客服人員對客戶的說法。

2. disclose Ⓥ 揭露

Please not to disclose anything information before the MOU is signed.

在簽 MOU 前,請不要揭示任何資訊。

3. evolution vs revolution 演進 vs 創新

在科技業中常聽到這兩個字,看起來差別不大,但其實兩者間有相當不同的解釋,Evolution 是種演進,根據目前已存在的加以改進,進而演變。Revolution 則是革命性的創新,是前所未見的全新東西。

4. all is said and done 不論如何;全盤考慮之後

When all is said and done, we can't reduce the number of teachers without lowering the quality of education.

不論如何,沒辦法減少老師人數而不降低教育的品質。

 句型解析

"electric grid" 本身就有大眾輸送電路的意思,"off the grid (power grid)" 被使用來說明自給自足的電路系統,由於網路的盛行,因此 "on the grid" 被用來描述透過網路與世界連結,而這幾年的網路廣泛應用,因為每個人的資料都在網路中竄流,不管信用卡消費、安全監控系統的錄影、FB、twitter、google+、照片/影片的分享,還有未來更多的穿戴裝置應用,都讓大家的個資成為可追蹤的資訊,因此常在電影或影片對話中

聽到 "on the grid" 的說法。由於無線通訊的使用，使每個用戶的行蹤，個人資料都被記錄，都可被追蹤，縱使你不想，也是無法避免。

 句型延伸及範例

1. What is the meaning of "everyone will be on the grid"？My favorite example of this is the movie "Enemy of the State".

「電子資訊監控」是什麼意思呢？我最喜歡的這個例子是電影「全民公敵」。

2. The boy wants to buy a computer to be on the grid.

這男孩想要買一台電腦，好透過網路來與世界連結。

What's Getting You Down?

什麼讓你心情不好？

 **Dialogue**

科技業無往不利的英語力

A: What's getting you down?

B: I was scolded by my boss for not doing things his way.

A: I am sorry. How often does it happen? Does he treat everyone the same?

B: Yes. It happens to everyone from time to time. It results from poor management, really. It's just a hostile working environment.

A: Have you spoken to the Human Resources Department about that? Would that help to escalate things?

B: I haven't decided whether or not to take that action. On the one hand, he is a moody person. We don't take these confrontations personally. On the other hand, I have learned many things from him.

 對話譯文

A： 什麼讓你心情不好？

B： 我被老闆罵沒有按照他要的方式做。

A： 我很抱歉。這發生的很頻繁嗎？他是對每個人都一樣？

B： 嗯，對每個人都一樣，偶而就發生。這原因是管理不當，是一個讓人覺得有敵意的工作環境。

A： 你曾與人力資源部門談過這個問題？向上申訴是不是會有些幫助呢？

B： 我還沒決定是否要這麼做。一方面，他只是一個喜怒無常的人，我們不認為這樣的衝突是針對個人。在另一方面，我從他身上學到很多的東西。

科技關鍵知識用語

1.**from time to time**　偶而，不定時 (=now and then)
Get up from your chair and stretch from time to time. Don't sit down for too long.
偶而就要從座位起來伸展一下，不要一直坐著。

2. hostile `adj` 有敵意的，不友善的

The book review she wrote is a very hostile criticism.

她寫的書評是非常不友善的批評。

3. escalate `v` 上升，升級

I like to escalate the issue for an immediate action.

我想提升問題的層級以獲得即時行動。

4. confrontation `n` 衝突

People usually dislike to deal with confrontation.

人們通常不喜歡面對衝突。

 句型解析

當看到別人心情不好，要如何安慰紓解對方，這裡有幾種說法。

1. 適合用來關心詢問他人的說法:

What's the matter?

怎麼回事？

Are you alright?

你還好嗎？

What's getting you down?

什麼讓你心情不好？

2. 有希望對方接下來告訴妳發生什麼事的說法

You look a bit down.

你看起來很糟糕。

3. 向對方表示同情的說法

Is there anything I can do to help?

我能為妳做什麼嗎？

4 外國人用這說法來表示對方遭遇重大棘手問題之後，建議對方讓自己心情緩和一下

You look like you could do with a drink.

看起來你需要喝一杯舒緩一下。

 句型延伸及範例

1. What's the matter? A cloud has come over your face.

怎麼回事？你看起來一臉烏雲密佈。

2. Is there anything I can do to help? Do you need a shoulder to cry on?

我能為妳做什麼嗎？要我的肩膀借你哭一下嗎？

I Wonder If You Could Help Me...?

不知你是否可以幫我……？

Dialogue

科技業無往不利的英語力

Boss: Come on in, Tom.

Tom: Our competitor launched a new model. I've already got one from the market.

Boss: Let's have a look! Are you able to set it up in my office? I like to see how this projector works in an environment like my office, a well-lighted room.

Tom: Let me connect the cable. **I wonder if you could help me** plug the power cord into the wall plug behind your chair.

Boss: Sure.

(A while later···)

Tom: There you go! It is on now. You know, the image looks quite vivid in an illuminated room.

Boss: So it does. We may be losing ground here.

 對話譯文

老闆： 進來吧，**Tom**。

Tom： 我們的競爭對手推出了新產品，我已經從市場上買了一台回來。

老闆： 讓我們一起來看看吧！你能把它在我的辦公室架好嗎？我想看看這台投影機在我這樣光線充足的辦公環境裡的表現如何。

Tom： 我把線連接好，不知道你能不能幫我把電源線插到你椅子後面的牆上？

老闆： 沒問題。

（過了一會兒……）

Tom： 這就好了，已經開機了。你看，它在明亮房間的投影結果相當鮮明。

老闆： 沒錯，我們可能會處於不利的地位。

科技關鍵知識用語

1. wall plug 牆上的電源插座

The wire snapped at the wall plug, and nearly started a fire.

牆上插座的電線短路了，還差一點引起火災。

2. illuminate v 照亮，啟發，啟蒙

Your observations have been illuminating.

你的觀察很有啟發性。

3. vivid adj （光、色）鮮明的，栩栩如生的

His speech was spiced with vivid examples.

他在演說中穿插了一些生動的例子。

4. lose ground 處於不利的地位；失去優勢

My company had lost ground after launching an unreliable product.

我們公司在上市一個不穩定的產品之後，失去了市場的優勢。

 句型解析

尋求協助的說法有很多，當需要老闆或權威人士幫忙時，該如何說才不至於失禮，**"I wonder if you could help me with this?"** 是禮貌的方式詢問對方是否能幫一下忙。相對的另一種比較直接的說法 **"I need some help, please."**，基本上這種說法，說話者不期待對方會說 **"no"**，通常是老闆和權威者對下屬的說法，所以別用錯囉！

句型延伸及範例

其他還有許多不同的說法，都是在尋求協助，但有不同的程度與情況背景：

1.Can you give me a hand with this?

～較不正式的說法，通常用於向你熟悉的人要求協助。

2.Could you spare a moment?

～當對方手上也在做某些事時，而你只需短暫協助時的說法。

3.Could you help me for a second?

～你只需小小幫忙時的說法。

4.Can I ask a favor?

～非常普遍的說法要求協助。

5.I can't manage this. Can you help?

～很強烈的方式告訴對方你無法處理手上的問題，真的需要幫忙。

MEMO

Where Do You Stand (on...)?

你對……的看法呢？

 **Dialogue**

科技業無往不利的英語力

Product leader: The current trend in the market is to offer lower cost models. The smartphone has come to a stage like commodity goods once did. Given the all-in-one chipsets designed by the suppliers, the entry barrier to enter the market is not what it was before. We can foresee much more competition in the near future, and much more fierce tactics.

R&D leader: Given our company's infrastructure, developing a budget-priced model doesn't take less time than developing something high end. Volume business is not on our plate.

Boss: I'd like to hear about this from a Sales point of view. **Where do you stand?**

Sales leader: Both of our colleagues make valid points from their unique angles. In a perfect situation we would prefer to sell both products. But given the real-word situation, I support the opinion of our R&D leader.

 對話譯文

產品負責人：銷售低價位產品是市場趨勢，智慧手機已經到了大眾商品相同的階段。由於供應商將所有功能設計在一個晶片裡，這讓進入這產業門檻不再是像從前那樣高，我們將可以看見更多的競爭者，以及更激烈的戰略。

研發負責人：以我們公司基礎設施情況，要研發生產一個低價位產品所需時間不會比高端型號短，以數量考量的業務模式不是我們的選擇。

老闆：我想聽聽從業務的角度，妳的看法呢？

業務負責人：他們兩位說的都正確，只是由自己不同的出發點來看。完美的情況下，我相信我們希望兩者都有。但在現實的世界裡，我同意研發負責人的意見。

WEEK 8

Where Do You Stand (on...)?

科技關鍵知識用語

1. trend 🔤 趨勢

The trend of prices is still upwards.

物價的趨向是仍在上漲。

2. entry barrier 進入障礙

The government has established significant entry barriers on international trade for warding off competition from outside.

政府架起顯著的國際貿易進入門檻以抵禦外來的競爭者。

3. volume business / high-volume business 大宗業務

The customer generally expects to receive a price discount on volume business.

客戶通常預期大量購買會有價格折扣。

4. infrastructure 🔤 基礎建設

Taipei city has built up very good infrastructure for international tourism.

台北市已經建立好很好的國際觀光基礎建設。

5. support / side with / take the side of 同意，支持，站在……的一邊

She sided with me against her family.

她支持我反對她的家人。

句型解析

詢問別人意見的說法有很多，可以對熟悉朋友的輕鬆非正式詢問方式，也有非常正式嚴肅的方式，適合在工作場合的討論中以直接方式詢問的說法是 **"Where do you stand(on...)?"** 或 **"What are your views on...?"**，兩者皆是詢問對方對此事的立場想法。

 句型延伸及範例

其他適合工作場合的說法

1. What would you say if we moved the microphones up by 1mm?

   我們把麥克風往上移 1mm，你認為如何？

   ～在討論中，這說法將想詢問的問題放在 **if** 之後的句子，而所用的動詞須是過去式，因是個假設語氣。

2. Are you aware of the resignation of our boss?

   你知道我們的老闆辭職的事嗎？

   ～雖這句話的詢問是關於老闆辭職的這事件，但詢問者這種問法其實是希望對方能對這事件發表看法和意見。

215

That Was a Bit Uncalled For

不需要這樣

 **Dialogue**

科技業無往不利的英語力

Daisy: Hi, Joseph. What's up? You look very depressed.

Joseph: Yes, I am left twisting in the wind. My supervisor is mad about the supplier I signed a contract with. This supplier has already missed the delivery schedule twice and it is creating big problems for our production. I am not sure what to do now. I might lose my job because of the bad decision I have made.

Daisy: Sorry to hear that.

Joseph: She even said something humiliating: her two-year-old son knows how to make better decisions than I did.

Daisy: <u>That was a bit uncalled for.</u>

 **對話譯文**

Daisy：嗨，**Joseph**。怎麼了？你看上去很沮喪。

Joseph：是的，我現在不知所措、孤立無援。我的老闆對我所簽下的供應商很生氣，因為他們已經兩次交貨不準時，造成我們生產上很大的問題。我不知道現在該怎麼辦，可能因為做這錯誤的決定而失去我的工作。

Daisy：很遺憾發生這些事。

Joseph：她甚至還說了一句很讓我丟臉的話，她說連她的兩歲的兒子都比我還知道如何做決定。

Daisy：她不須這樣說話。

科技關鍵知識用語

1.twist in the wind (left hanging)　孤立無援

The rebellion kid got left twisting in the wind. Looks like his parents have given up on him this time.

這叛逆的孩子現在孤立無援。看起來這次連他的父母都放棄他了。

2.humiliating　adj　羞辱的；丟臉的

It was very humiliating I forgot completely what to say during the presentation. My mind went blank back then for a few minutes.

很丟臉在簡報中我完全忘了該說些什麼。有幾分鐘我的腦子裡一片空白。

 句型解析

在工作場合中，不論是在一對一或是會議當中，有些人對有些事不滿意很有可能進而對人的批評說出無理、具有人身攻擊性的話語，尤其在工作場合多多少少你可能會碰到對方說話非常不得體，不恰當的情況。如何對這情況用適當不帶情緒的方式表達對方態度的不得宜：**It was a bit un-called for.**（uncalled-for: 不需要，不恰當，不合適），沒有情緒字眼就能完全詮釋。

句型延伸及範例

1. I am not a fan of our new manager, but Mark's comments about him at the meeting were a bit uncalled for.

   我對新來的經理沒什麼好感，但Mark不須在會議中對他下這樣的評論。

2. A: Hey, your co-worker looks fat and ugly.
   B: That is a bit uncalled for.

   A：嘿，你的同事看起來又胖又醜。

   B：你有點過分。

2. Your criticism of John in the meeting was a bit uncalled for.

   你在會議中對John的批評有點超過。

MEMO

WEEK 8

That Was a Bit Uncalled For

I'm
Not at Liberty to...

我無權……

科技業無往不利的英語力

 **Dialogue**

Tim: Hi Helen. Unusual to see you in office at this hour. Busy?

Helen: It is near year end. We are busy trying to close the financial books.

Tim: How have we been doing this quarter? Lately, our company's share price has been looking stagnant. I want to buy a new car and I've been watching for the opportunity to sell my shares at a good price.

Helen: **I'm not at the liberty to** release any financial information before the business review meeting. But you should be able to get a sense of things yourself, given how many projects your team is working on.

Tim: Thanks. That is right!

 對話譯文

Tim： **Helen** 你好。很不尋常在這個時候看到你在辦公室。很忙嗎？

Helen： 接近年底，我們忙著結帳。

Tim： 我們這一季的營收如何啊？最近，我們公司的股價看起來好像有點停止不動。我想買一輛車，想等好價格賣掉我的一些股票。

Helen： 在業績檢討報告前，我不能告訴你任何財務信息。但看看你們團隊在忙的這麼多案子，你應該能夠自己判斷。

Tim： 謝謝。沒錯！

科技關鍵知識用語

1. close the financial book 結帳

Don't talk too loud and bother your dad, he's struggling to close the financial book.

講話不要太大聲也不要去煩你爸爸，他正忙著結帳。

2. stagnant [adj] 停滯

The market is extremely stagnant.

市場極為蕭條。

科技業無往不利的英語力

 句型解析

"liberty"的中文意思是自由，"at liberty" 解釋為能自由做某些事，**"I'm not at liberty to say…"** 解釋為我沒又這個權利或我沒有被授權去説。當你被詢問到一些機密資訊不方便説，或你所在的職務並不適合發表意見及透露訊息時，則可用，**"I'm not at the liberty to say."** 或 **"Sorry, it is confidential."** 。

拒絕提供資訊的情況有很多，不同情況可有不同回答。**"no comment"** 通常用於政治問題或對媒體的答覆。**"Let me get back to you"** 在工作上也常用到，但這情況則是你可能需確認或你不知道答案，需要些時間再答覆對方。

句型延伸及範例

1. I'm not at the liberty to discuss this with you.

   我沒權利與你討論這個問題。

2. He is not at the liberty to disclose the information.

   他沒有立場透露這訊息。

3. You are at the liberty to go anywhere you wish.

   你可自由地去任何你想去的地方。

MEMO

WEEK 8

I'm Not at Liberty to…

Get Up on the Wrong Side of Bed

心情莫名地不好

 **Dialogue**

Wilson: Hi, Allan. Did you just come out from boss's office? Do you happen to know whether he is available now?

Allan: Yes, I'm pretty sure he is available. I just finished meeting with him. But I hope you are bringing some good news. Looks like our boss <u>got up on the wrong side of the bed</u> this morning.

Wilson: Oh, he is in a bad mood. I guess I will report first the deal we just successfully closed. I'll bring up the project schedule delay issue later. Thanks for the heads up!

 對話譯文

Wilson：嗨，**Allan**。你剛剛從老闆的辦公室出來嗎？你知道他現在是否在忙嗎？

Allan：我非常確定他現在有空，我剛跟他開完會。但我希望你帶來的是些好消息。他看起來心情莫名地不好。

Wilson：哦，他心情不好了。我想我先報告我們成功拿到案子的好消息，再提其他案子進度落後的問題。謝謝你的警告。

 科技關鍵知識用語

1.**Do you happen to know**⋯ 你會不會剛好知道⋯⋯
Do you happen to know how to get to the subway station?
是否剛好你知道如何去地鐵站？

2.**bad mood** 心情不好（前面加 **in**）
She is in a bad mood.
她心情不好。

moody `adj` 表示心情多變、情緒化

Tyler's mother is very moody, and she is very difficult to deal with.

Tyler的媽媽很情緒化，是個很難打交道的人。

3. **heads up**　提醒，警告

I wanted to give you the heads up that I'll be sending you the payment tomorrow.

我想先提醒你明天我會付款。

  句型解析

在工作場所中，如何用沒有情緒或不具有人身攻擊的方式來描述一些具有情緒的情況，對英文是第二語言的商務人士來說，這需要特別去學習，本書中提供了幾種不同情況的應對說法。

在這裡 **"get up on the wrong side of bed"** 是形容某人今天心情不好，可能是你的老闆或共事的同事，有點莫名怒氣的態度或說話不合情理的火爆，是一種戲謔方式來說明某人莫名地心情不好，也就是我們中文裡所說的「起床氣」。

句型延伸及範例

1. Did you get up on the wrong side of bed? Are you in a bad mood? Should I come back later?

   你起錯床了嗎？心情不好？我是否等一下再來呢？

   ～不適合對上級或不熟的人如此對話

2. A: She is in a grouchy and cranky mood.

   B: Her son went to the hospital emergency room last night.

   A：她今天老是發牢騷，心情古怪。

   B：她的兒子昨晚去醫院掛急診。

3. I had a bumper accident this morning on my way to work. I got off to a bad start today.

   我今天早上，在上班路上出了個小車禍，一早就出師不利。

MEMO

Out of Reach

Dialogue

A: Did you see the news today? Our competitor has successfully managed to step into the car industry. They have demonstrated a prototype connected vehicle. It looks awesome.

B: Indeed it does. It's very cool, but I believe the price will be **out of reach** for most of car buyers. It will be a niche product. To prevail in the mass market will take some time. A connected vehicle still falls into the luxury car category, after all.

A: Nevertheless, sooner or later the price will fall into an affordable range for most consumers. Have you thought about going into that field yourself?

B: If a chance arises, why not? But before then I will need to brush up my wireless credentials and expand my skill set.

科技業無往不利的英語力

 對話譯文

A：你看到今天的新聞嗎？我們的競爭對手已經成功跨入汽車產業，他們示範了新的無線連結車的模型。看起來真棒。

B：確實如此，看起來很酷，但我相信它的價格對大多數的購車族仍是遙不可及的，會是一個小眾產品。要盛行還需要一段時間，畢竟目前仍然屬於豪華車範疇。

A：不過，遲早價格會在可接受的範圍。你會考慮進入那產業嗎？

B：如果有機會的話，當然。不過在這之前，我還需要精進我的無線技術領域的相關技能。

 科技關鍵知識用語

1. niche product　小眾產品

We like to focus on the margin we can make. Therefore, we make niche products.

利潤是我們的訴求，所以我們生產小眾有利基的產品。

科技業無往不利的英語力

2. prevail v 戰勝，主宰，盛行

The public interests prevail over an individual's.

公眾利益遠駕於個人之上。

3. nevertheless adv 不論如何

It is a small but nevertheless important change.

雖然是個小的改變，但不論如何是個很重要的改變。

4. sooner or later 早晚

Sooner or later, children will leave their parents and have their own life.

小孩早晚會離開父母，過他們自己的生活。

5. affordable adj 買得起

The property in Taipei is not affordable for most of the people.

台北的房產對大部分人都是買不起的。

6. brush up 精進（技術，知識）

I need to brush my English up.

我必須精進我的英文。

7. skill set 技能組合

We are looking for someone with good communication and problem solving skill set.

我們在找同時具有溝通和解決問題技能組合的人。

句型解析

"reach" 一個字，用於動詞的中文翻譯一般較常使用是「到達」，但當名詞時常常用來形容「取得」，**"out of reach"** 則是「不可觸及」、「遙不可及」，通常表示一個目標或一件物品是遙不可及的。平常生活中最常見的則有在藥瓶外的標示可看到 **"keep it out of reach of children"**「置於小孩無法取得之處」。

句型延伸及範例

1. A tour to Mars soon will not be out of reach.

   去火星之旅很快不再是遙不可及。

2. We don't make attention-grabbing but expensive products that are out of reach of real consumers. We do a volume business

   不要做一個價格遙不可及的叫好產品，我們對大量銷售的生意比較有興趣。

It's Unlikely/Likely That...

這不太可能（很有可能）……

Dialogue

科技業無往不利的英語力

Luis: Jonathan, may I talk to you for a few seconds?

Jonathan: Sorry. I am very tied up now. May I come over to look for you in half an hour?

Luis: Sure.

(A while later···)

Jonathan: Sorry to keep you waiting. May I know what this is about?

Luis: I have just received a change request from the customer for the model your team is responsible for. The mass production schedule remains the same.

Jonathan: I am afraid **that is very unlikely** we will be able to agree on terms. First, the hardware layout is frozen. No more changes are allowed except for minor modifications. Any major change in hardware will result in a schedule delay and involve some cost.

 對話譯文

Luis：**Jonathan**，我可以和你談一下嗎？

Jonathan：對不起。我現在正忙，半小時後我去找你好嗎？

Luis：好的。

（過了一會兒……）

Jonathan：不好意思，讓你久等了。什麼事呢？

Luis：我剛剛收到客戶要求對你的團隊負責的產品做些變更，並且要求量產時間保持不變。

Jonathan：恐怕不太可能同意這麼做。首先，硬體設計已固定，沒辦法變更，只能些微的小修改。任何在硬體上的重大變化將會影響量產時程，還會有成本產生。

科技關鍵知識用語

1.I am very tied up 我目前手中正有事忙著

"tied up" 而用於形容人的時候則是指「忙得不可開交」或是「脫不了身」。

2.half an hour 半小時

注意：不是 half hour，此為常見錯誤。

3.result in 造成，產生

The air plane crash resulted in the deaths of 14 passengers.

飛機墜毀造成 14 人喪生。

 句型解析

"**It's unlikely/likely that...**" 用於推測的說法上，對於結果未明，但心中已有較確定的答案時使用。對某些事我們無法確定是否發生而必須做出猜測，根據情況有許多不同程度的說法。

1. 比較確定的說法

"No doubt…" 「不用懷疑，一定會……」

2. 說法是較不確定，可能是 50-50 的機率

"In all probability, it will…" 「有可能的話，應該……」

"The chances are that…" 「有機會的話……」

3. 比較不可能的意思

"It's unlikely that…" 「不太可能……」

"There's only a chance that…" 「有一點可能……」

"I wouldn't be surprised if…" 「若……我不會驚訝」（不太可能發生，但若發生也不驚訝。）

1. No doubt she will nail it.

   毫無疑問，她會做到。

2. It's unlikely that we can make it tomorrow.

   不可能我們明天能做好。

3. In all probability, he will join us.

   有可能他將加入我們的行列。

4. There's only a slim chance that he will win the election.

   只有一點可能他會贏得選舉。

Whichever Is the Case...

不論任何情況……

Dialogue

科技業無往不利的英語力

A: The reason I called the meeting today is to discuss with you a new product category we are now aiming to create: commercial drones. Many of you might wonder whether we can acquire the expertise to do this, as our current product line is rather far from this field.

However, my purpose is not to argue for it. Instead, I'd like to hear each of you discuss the best ways we may prepare for this and kick it off.

As we know, commercial drones can take part in a number of industries: agriculture, energy, utilities, mining, construction, real estate, wildlife conservation, news media and film production.

<u>Whichever is the case</u> you choose to examine, I would like to see a pros-and-cons report from you. Then we will explore how best we may proceed. Any question?

B: I think we are all delighted to do feasibility study for getting into new category.

 對話譯文

A：我今天找你們來開這個會，主要是有關我們計劃要做的新產品，就是商用無人駕駛飛行器。你們之中許多人可能會問我們是否有這技術，因為目前我們的產品線跟這領域有點遠。不過，今天的目的不是要爭論這個問題，而是我希望你們每個人都能討論我們需要做哪些準備才能開始。我們都知道，商用無人駕駛飛行器的應用領域有很多：農業、能源、公用事業、礦業、建築、房地產、野生動物保護，新聞媒體和電影製作。無論是你能想到的任何例子，我希望大家能給我你對此計畫利與弊的看法，從大家的報告中，我們看看該如何進行。還有問題嗎？

B：我想大家都很高興能參與進入新產業的可行性研究。

科技關鍵知識用語

1. aim ⓥ 瞄準目標，打算

I aim to include all the employees to go for the training tomorrow.

我打算讓所有員工參加明天的培訓。

2. expertise ⓝ 專業

That is not my area of expertise.

那是非我專業領域。

3. a number of 許多

Our guests are coming from a number of different countries.

我們的賓客來自許多不同國家。

4. pros-and-cons 優缺點

Please be reminded. A pros-and-cons analysis should be included in whatever subject you touch on in your study.

請注意，不論你們的研究主題是什麼，都要包括優缺點分析。

 句型解析

"Whichever is the case..." 「不論任何情況」意指你所說的聲明都適用於你所說的許多不同選擇中，其他的取代用法有，"in any case" 和 "at any rate"，"whichever the case may be"。

句型延伸及範例

1. Whichever the case may be, you should apologize.

   不管是什麼情況，你都應道歉。

2. A surgical training takes 5, 7 or 9 years. Whichever is the case, it is an extremely challenging journey.

   外科培訓需要5、7或9年。無論是什麼情況，這是一個極具挑戰的旅程。

MEMO

You Could Be Right, but...

您可能沒錯，但……

Dialogue

科技業無往不利的英語力

Customer: We like the commercial drones you just demonstrated. But we have calculated that the noise emission exceeds regulations. Are you able to make some adjustments to reduce it? Such as reducing the voltage?

Supplier: **You could be right, but** noise results from more than voltage. We began by making industrial drones for manufacturing, so noise control in the product is less sensitive than on commercial drones. Knowing the difference in those two categories, we recently set up a new team to test drones for commercial use. We expect to see some new designs in three months.

Customer: That is great. I think we are very interested to see your new product line.

對話譯文

客戶：我們很喜歡你們剛才展示的商用無人飛行器。但我發現它的噪音值超出了規定範圍。你能夠做一些調整嗎？譬如降低電壓？

供應商：您的建議可能沒錯，但要降低噪音值的調整不只是電壓的問題。我們過去做工業用無人飛行器製造，產品的噪音控制比商業使用來的寬鬆。我們瞭解這兩者的差異，所以已經成立了另一團隊來設計商業用無人飛行器，預計 3 個月後可看到新產品。

客戶：太好了，我們對你們的新的產品線非常有興趣。

科技關鍵知識用語

1. results from　因……而造成

The failure results from poor planning and reckless action.

失敗源自於很糟的計畫和魯莽的行動。

2. knowing　adj　知道

Knowing you are coming, I have spared a seat for you.

知道你要來，我留了一個位子給你。

句型解析

如何對別人的意見表示反對？可以是非常直接無遮掩的表示反對，

例如

> I don't agree with your opinion. / I disagree.

但若加入一些修飾則可軟化反對的態度，讓人聽起來較不至於咄咄逼人。

例如

> I am afraid I don't agree."

當需要用間接方式來表達反對別人意見時，例如對話中提及的 **"you could be right, but..."** 或是 **"I am not so sure about that!"**，這兩種表達都是用較有禮貌的方式來表示反對。

若只是對部分論點反對，可以說：

★ I agree up to a point, but I think…

★ What you have said is an interesting idea, but I think…

要記住，需依據場合和對話者的身分立場來選擇適合的表達方式。

1. I am afraid I disagree with your statement simply because we lack any data to support that idea.

   恐怕我無法同意你所說的，僅因我們缺乏數據來支持你的論點。

2. You could be right in making that observation, but at the time we entered, we saw a completely different scenario.

   你的觀察或許是對的，但當我們走進來時，我們所見是完全不同的情景。

3. I agree up to a point, but I think people will have concerns if they wear a garment with electronic chipsets embedded.

   我只同意某些部分，但我認為人們對穿戴著嵌有電子晶片的服裝會有所顧慮。

Give It One's Best Shot!

盡……最大的努力！

科技業無往不利的英語力

 Dialogue

Morris: Steve, I have seen your proposal for the pricing strategy. We will offer that to our biggest client as they prepare a purchase plan for next year.

You nailed it! I gave it thumbs up and passed it on to the financial department for execution.

Steve: Thanks for your support, Morris. I am meeting the client tomorrow and expect a long day as usual.

Morris: **Give it your best shot!** You can do it.

 對話譯文

Morris： **Steve**，我看到你提出的定價策略企畫書。我們將會提供給我們最大的客戶，讓他們準備明年他們的採購計劃。

你抓到了重點，寫得很好！我已核准並送到財務部門請他們執行。

Steve： **Morris**，感謝您的支援。我明天會跟客戶開會，又將是個冗長的談判大賽。

Morris： 盡你最大的努力！你沒問題的。

 科技關鍵知識用語

1. nail it 抓到重點，搞定了
You have nailed it. Well done!
你完全正確，抓到重點了。做得好！

科技業無往不利的英語力

2.**a thumb up**　同意

The board of directors has given her promotion a thumb up.

董事會已同意她的升職。

 句型解析

<u>"Give it your best shot!"</u> 的意思為「盡你最大的努力！」，而如何對工作夥伴、下屬給於鼓勵的說法，這裡提供一些不同程度、不同情況的使用：

1.**Keep up the good work!**

　繼續保持。

　（已經做得很好的狀況下。）

2.**You're on the right track.**

　做的沒錯。

　（鼓勵其繼續努力）

3.**Keep going. / Come on, you can do it.**

　勇往直前。／你辦得到的。

　（有加油打氣，鼓勵其不要放棄的意味！）

4.**What have you got to lose?**

　有啥好損失的？

　（當對方猶豫不決時，鼓勵他試試看，沒什麼損失）

句型延伸及範例

1. Alice, get on deck. Give it your best shot!

   Alice 妳是下一個。盡妳最大的努力！

   （ "on deck" 源自於球賽，下一位球員在等候區等待上場。）

2. If I were you, I would take the offer to work overseas. What have you got to lose?

   如果我是妳，我會接受這個到海外工作的機會。妳有什麼好損失的嗎？

MEMO

Does It Ring a Bell?

有印象了嗎？

科技業無往不利的英語力

 **Dialogue**

Cecelia: Hi, Sam. I'm so surprised to see you here!

Sam: I'm sorry. Have we met?

Cecelia: Yes! I am Cecelia. Our company sells wireless charging modules. Three months ago we visited your company and made a presentation to you and your group. **Does it ring a bell?**

Sam: Of course. Absolutely. Our people were all very impressed with your solution. Unfortunately, we decided to go with a different standard in designing our new product.

Cecelia: No problem at all! If your team ever decides to make a switch, remember we are still here for you.

對話譯文

Cecelia：嗨，Sam，想不到會在這裡看到你！

Sam：不好意思，我們見過面嗎？

Cecelia：是啊，我是 Cecelia。我們公司銷售的無線充電模組，3 個月前我們曾拜訪貴公司並為你的團隊做了簡報。有印象嗎？

Sam：噢……對，當然我記得，我們都對貴公司提供的產品非常印象深刻。不幸的是，我們決定用另外的不同規格來設計產品。

Cecelia：沒問題的！如果你的團隊有一天想換，我們樂意為您服務。

 科技關鍵知識用語

當被不認識的人叫住時，要如何反應才不致失禮？

★ **Have we met?**

我們見過面嗎？/我們認識嗎？

（這是很有禮貌的答覆方式。）

★ Do I know you?

我認識你嗎？

（稍微較不正式，較適用於同輩或年輕人。）

★ Who are you?

你是誰？

（不要用此方式回答，尤其在工作場合，會讓對方感覺尷尬。）

科技業無往不利的英語力

💡 句型解析

"**Does it ring a bell?**"用來說「你有印象嗎？」、「記得嗎？」，提醒某人過去的人、事、物。有時你會聽到 "**Does it ring any bell?**" 這也是同樣意思，但有細微差別。加 "**any**" 時，來強調你認為這件事物對這個人應該是不會不記得的。

而若真的還是不記得，你的回答可以是：

Sorry. I have no memory of meeting you.

「不好意思，我真的沒印象見過你。」

I'm afraid it doesn't ring a bell.

「恐怕我真的不記得。」

I've completely forgotten.

「我完全沒印象。」

當有人問你是否有印象答應做某事，而你忘了，回答則可是：

Oh no, it completely slipped my mind.

「喔，糟糕，我把它拋在腦後了。」

 句型延伸及範例

1. That name rings a bell and I think I've met him.

   我對這名字有印象，我想我見過他。

2. Does the name 'Alan Ma' ring a bell?

   Alan Ma 這名字你有印象嗎？

3. I'm sorry, your description doesn't ring any bells with me.

   不好意思，你的描述，我一點印象都沒有。

MEMO

As Far As Someone Is Concerned...

就……對這件事的看法而言

 **Dialogue**

A: In light of many recent incidents of credit card fraud, now is a good time to explore ways to protect and secure our money. Mobile payment seems to be inevitable and NFC is the entry ticket into the game. I'd say it's time we caught that rising tide and became a part of it, but I'd like to hear your opinion.

B: I agree with your suggestion. We need to do something about the security issues, no doubt. **As far as I am concerned**, mobile payment is inevitable anyway. We may as well plan to make the shift.

A: Mobile payment offers us a security solution but we face the problem of convincing users. Mobile payment is safe and hassle free when used with double validation. The transaction has to be validated by your fingerprint and a separate secure element chip that is embedded into the device.

科技業無往不利的英語力

WEEK 9

As Far As Someone Is Concerned...

 對話譯文

A： 有鑑於近來許多的信用卡詐騙，現在是一個很好的時機推出一種可確保我們的錢不會被輕易偷竊的解決方案。移動支付似乎是不可避免的趨勢，而 NFC 則是進入此遊戲的門票。乘著上升的趨勢，我們不可在此一機會中缺席。我想聽聽你對進入這領域的意見。

B： 我同意你的建議。毫無疑問我們必須解決安全性的考量。就我對這件事的看法而言，行動支付不可避免，我們最好計畫如何轉型。

A： 我認為已有解決安全考量的方案，但重點是如何讓使用者信服。手機支付是安全無慮的，使用雙重的驗證：交易必須通過用戶指紋和獨立嵌入的安全元件晶片的驗證來批准的流程。

 科技關鍵知識用語

1.in light of 　根據（數據或得到的資訊）

In light of what you have told us, I think we must reconsider about our strategy.

根據你所說的，我們必須重新考慮我們的策略。

2. **inevitable** adj 無法避免

To reduce the number of our retail shops is an inevitable conclusion.

減少我們的零售點是無法避免的結論。

3. **rising tide** 漲潮; 這一波大趨勢

He caught the rising tide to jump into the gold trading business. Now he has made a fortune.

他把握趨勢，進入黃金買賣生意，現在賺了一大筆錢。

4. **validation** n 驗證，生效，確實
validate v

After we validate your password and the key you have, you may open your safe box in our bank.

在我們驗證你的密碼和手上鑰匙後，你就可打開在我們銀行的保險箱。

 句型解析

分享自己意見時，小心不要將自己意見用陳述真理的態度和語氣來表達，可能會讓人反感，說服力受打折。

而表達意見也有許多不同方式，這裡使用的 "As far as I am concerned..." 「就我對這件事看法而言」是要表達對這主題帶有負面的警示意見。

其他分享意見的說法還有：

★ If you don't mind me saying...

如果你不介意，我認為⋯⋯

★ I'm utterly convinced that...
我完全的被説服，我認為……

★ In my humble opinion...
依我的淺見，我認為……

 句型延伸及範例

1.A far as the mayor is concerned, the stadium project doesn't comply with safety regulations regardless of how breath-taking the architecture looks. He has decides to halt the construction.

就市長的想法而言，體育場的工程不符合安全規範，不管它的建築設計如何讓人驚艷，他決定要停止建造。

2.If you don't mind me saying, your opinion doesn't represent for all of us.

如果你不介意，我認為你的意見並不代表我們所有人的。

3.I'm utterly convinced that she will have to veto the bill.

我完全同意，她將必須否決該法案。

4.In my humble opinion, I think we let the issue drop for now and revisit it at a later date.

這是我的淺見，我認為我們現在先將這個問題放一邊，日後再回來看。

I've Not Given It Much Thought...

我還沒思考這個問題……

 **Dialogue**

A: Have you all paid attention to the news lately? Convergent products are happening in many different industries, from textiles to automobiles. When people say "Internet of Things" is the next big thing, they are actually referring to all the many different kinds of applications that will be built on wireless connection. At our last meeting, I requested that you all think about what kinds of convergent products we can explore and perhaps expand into. What is your opinion?

B: To be honest, **I've not given it much thought about**, simply because the resource we have on hand now are barely enough to sustain our core business. To enter a new field, I believe we will need more than just an idea of what we would like to do.

 對話譯文

A：你最近又看到一些新聞嗎？技術結合的產品在許多不同的產業都看的到，從紡織到汽車。當大家說「物聯網」是下一個蓬勃發展的大事實，這實際上是指許多不同類型的產品與無線傳輸的應用組合，上次會議我提到你是否能想想我們有什麼樣的產品可以進一步探討的。你有什麼想法嗎？

B：老實說，我還沒花時間去想這件事，只是因為現在我們手上的資源，只勉強夠完成我們現在手上的核心業務，若想進入另一個新的領域，我相信我們需要的不僅僅是做什麼產品的想法。

 科技關鍵知識用語

1. Internet of Things (IoT)   物聯網
很多不同人對它有不同解釋，但都有共通的涵義，就是在我們的世界裡，任何事物都能以有智慧的方式交流溝通。也就是説，由於物聯網，這實際的物理世界裡成為一個巨大相連資訊系統，不再只是電腦、平板、手機的連接運用而已。

2. sustain **v** 支援，承受，維持
His income can barely sustain the living of his family.

他的收入只能勉強維持家人的生活。

 句型解析

當被問到你的意見、看法時，在各種不同情況下，如何回答才能正確表達卻又不失禮，這裡提供的例子："I've not given it much thought." 「我還沒思考這問題」，這種回答可能是對這問題沒有太大興趣，會沒太多時間去想這問題。

在工作場合中，上層有時會有許多的創意或想法希望員工們加以思考，然而常常又是在現實情況下，對員工而言這些構想並不是眼前最急迫的問題，該如何適當表達自己的立場，這時可說 "I've not been able to give it much thought" 用 not be able to 表示較有禮貌的語氣。

 句型延伸及範例

1.A: I suspect that this year Ethan's team is more likely to get the salary bonus than our team is. What do you think?

B: Your guess is as good as mine.

A：我認為今年 Ethan 團隊的薪資獎金會比我們的多，你認為呢？

B：大概是吧！

～這種說法表示其實你對這件事沒有比對方知道得更多，無法加以判斷。

2.A: Look at the new smartwatch the Apple is launching, I believe demand for the wearable tech will take off dramatically. What do you think?

B: I couldn't agree with you more.

A：看到蘋果推出的智慧手錶，我相信穿戴技術的需求將顯著增加。你怎麼看？

B：我非常同意。

～這種說法表示你百分之百同意。

3.A: The company is going to expand and recruit some experts from among our competitors. Perhaps we will have a new boss. What do you think?

B: It doesn't make any difference to me.

A：公司準備要擴大規模及從競爭對手那兒挖角幾個專家。或許我們將會有個新老闆。你怎麼看呢？

B：這對我而言沒什麼差別。

～這種說法表示你對這主題其實沒太大意見。

I've Not Given It Much Thought...

The Odds Are...

有機會⋯⋯

 **Dialogue**

Sara: Hi, Patrick. I am calling to find out if it's possible to get the shipment out tomorrow. As you know, it takes tons of paperwork to get the process done. I would like to begin making arrangements at my end now if I will need to prepare that much paperwork tomorrow.

Earlier this morning, I talked to the Product Manager, though. She told me the de-bugging driver will not be released to factory until very late. It sounds to me as if the chance of a shipment tomorrow is small.

Patrick: I have made plans to work overtime tonight to refresh the software. The rest of the logistical arrangements can be made tomorrow. **The odds are** the shipment can be ready to go by 3:00 pm tomorrow.

 對話譯文

Sara：嗨，**Patrick**。我打電話來瞭解我們是否有機會明天讓貨出去。你知道出貨前還有一大堆檔要做，我想知道是否現在我就該開始準備，以免明天有一大堆事要做。

早先我跟產品經理聊過，她說解決一個產品問題的驅動程式很晚才會被核准發送到工廠，照這聽起來，明天出貨機會似乎很小。

Patrick：我已經準備好產線今晚加班灌軟體，其他的後勤安排可以明天做。所以有機會這批貨明天下午 **3** 點前可準備好。

科技關鍵知識用語

1. the chance is small　機會很小

Her chance of winning the business contract is small.

她拿到這生意合約的機會很小。

2. overtime　n　加班

We don't punch a clock at our work. Therefore, we don't get overtime pay.

我們上班不打卡，所以也沒加班費。

 科技業無往不利的英語力

 句型解析

odds：勝算，希望，可能性

一種對事情發生的機率的說法，依情況的不同也有許多不同的表達方式，從不太可能到非常可能，除了我們常用的"**very possible**"「非常有可能」和 "**very unlikely**"「非常不可能」之外，還有許多不同的說法。"**The odds are…**"的說法通常表示你認為事情發生的機率頗高。

1. It's probably we will have to go on the business trip tomorrow.

   明天很有可能我們要出差。

   另一種類似程度的說法：
   There's a good chance we will go on a business trip tomorrow.

2. I wouldn't be surprised if he comes for help tomorrow.

   我不驚訝如果明天他來找我們幫忙。

   ～這種說法的程度大約是一半一半的機率。

3. There's just a chance we have to start it over again.

   我們需要重頭作的機會不高。

   ～這種說法表示程度不高。

I Would Go for...

我肯定會……

 **Dialogue**

A: Wow, have you seen the news today? The big guys have launched their smartwatch line. The prices range from US$350 to US$17,000. I saw the video. The high-end watch looks chic and sleek, with fine metal chain band. That one could affect the market for fine Swiss watches, I think.

B: Are you sure? Many people will find it absurd to spend US$17,000 on a mini-computer that will be out of date in a couple of years. I would go for a traditional, finely crafted international brand watch.

 對話譯文

A： 哇，你看過今天的新聞嗎？這個大公司已經推出了他們的智慧型手錶，售價從 350 美元到 17,000 美元。在影片中，高檔的型號產品外觀看起來很時尚、別出心裁，金屬錶帶非常精緻，我想這會對瑞士製造的手錶造成影響。

B： 你確定嗎？花高於一萬塊美金買一個高科技手錶，過一段時間後就過時的高科技產品，我認為這很荒謬。用這些錢，如果可以選擇，我肯定買傳統的國際大品牌手錶。

科技關鍵知識用語

1. **sleek and chic** adj 時尚和別緻
   常常用來形容時尚產品

2. **absurd** adj 不合理的，荒謬的
   His plan was absurd, and bound to lead to catastrophe.
   他的計劃很荒謬，肯定會導致災難。
   ★ **catastrophe** n 災難

265

3. out of date   已經不流行的，過時的(=Outdated)

The high-tech gadget will go out of date in a couple of years.

這個高科技的配件在幾年內就會過時了。

科技業無往不利的英語力

 句型解析

"**I would go for…**"是用於表達自己的喜好及選擇，而需要表達喜好選擇的方式和程度也許多不同的説法，正式和非正式也有差別。不同程度的表達則大致可分為下面幾種：

★ 直接肯定的説出自己喜好，但當加上 **much** 之後，語氣是更強烈。

I would (much) prefer to…

I would (much) rather…

★ 這兩句的表達方式告訴對方他僅喜歡這個選擇。

I'd go for…

I much prefer…

★ 禮貌的表達方式，也説明是否依照他的喜好並不重要。

If it was up to me, I'd choose…

★ 説出自己喜好，但若其他人決定不同選擇，也沒關係。

Given the choice, I'd rather…

句型延伸及範例

1. I would much prefer to work with that design house that presented the open space idea for the showcase area.
我非常的喜歡提出用開放的空間理念為展示區概念的那家設計公司。

2. I would go for the second option, definitely.
我肯定會選擇第二個選項。

3. Given the choices, I would rather buy an iPhone.
如果可以選擇，我寧願買 iPhone。

I'm Afraid That's Not Quite Right

恐怕你的認知有所誤解……

 **Dialogue**

科技業無往不利的英語力

A: Please allow me to recap what we have just discussed. The lead time for introducing a new color feature for your model MA90, we have decided, is around 45 days.

There is no need for us to pay for the engineering cost of making a different color as long as we agree that you can offer the same color product to other customers.

B: You are right for most of the points, but **I'm afraid** the lead time calculation <u>is not quite right.</u> It is 45 days from the date you approve the sample result that we test and experiment with the color on the device.

對話譯文

A： 請讓我將我們剛才的討論複誦一遍。將你的產品型號 MA90 改變成我們想要的顏色所需的交貨時間大約是 45 天。

而且，我們沒有需要負責改變顏色所衍生的工程費用，只要我們同意你們可將此顏色產品提供其他客戶使用。

B： 你說的大部分都對，但恐怕你對交貨時間的計算方式有所誤解，是從我們的在產品上使用不同顏色測試結果獲得你們的核准之日起算 45 天。

 科技關鍵知識用語

1. **please allow me…** 請允許（讓）我……
Please allow me to make this straight.
請允許我直接了當把這說清楚。

2. **recap** v / n 重述
This is the recap of what we have agreed.
這是我們所同意的重述。

269

句型解析

當聽到某人所說的話是錯誤的或在對話過程中對方誤會你的意思，如何指出讓對方知道，這裡有幾種不同方式，分別表現出不同的語氣強弱程度。

1. **"I'm afraid that's not quite right…"**：「恐怕你的認知有所誤解……」是種有禮貌的表達方式。

2. "I'm afraid you're mistaken."：「恐怕你弄錯了。」，這樣的語氣則較上句稍微強些。

3. "No, you've got it wrong." 和" No, that's all wrong."：這樣的語氣則強很多，這種說法很可能引起對方不滿，應注意如此使用是否恰當。

科技業無往不利的英語力

句型延伸及範例

1. I am afraid your understanding is not quite right.

   恐怕你的理解不完全正確。

2. I am afraid you are mistaken about the complaint from the customers.

   我怕你對客戶的投訴有所誤解。

3. You have got it all wrong about the message the data revealed.

   你對數據透露的訊息完全搞錯了。

MEMO

運動週
Win by a Nose

以些微差距勝出

運動週

商業上的競爭和運動的競爭有其相當大的相似之處，因此在對話上常用運動的專有說法來描述商業行為。尤其是在與美國客戶或同事的對話時，常會出現。

當面對外國客戶和同事時，是否對他們的一些說法摸不著頭腦呢？本書的這周用語，針對常用於工作場合的運動用語對話加以說明，讓你輕而易舉了解對話，不須猜測對方意思。

Dialogue

Michael: Dirk, we just came back from the sample evaluation meeting with the mobile operator. After running neck-and-neck with the competition for weeks, we finally **won by a nose**.

Dirk: That's great. Fill me in, please.

Michael: At the end, they told me about the process they went through. In addition to the basic phone functions, the evaluation team focused on the multimedia performance of all the devices. Although our handset performed slightly less reliably than we had hoped in the phone function, it tested as slightly faster and more stable on the video streaming program they plan to launch. We barely won the gig.

 對話譯文

Michael：**Dirk**，我們剛剛從運營商的樣品評估會議回來，與對手經過幾個星期不相上下的評估之後，我們以些微差距贏得這個案子。

Dirk：太好了，請告訴我情況。

Michael：結束後，他們告訴我評估的過程，除了基本的電話功能外，焦點放在每個電話樣品的多媒體性能表現。雖然我們的產品電話功能稍有不足，但對營運商將要推出影片在線觀看的計劃上，我們產品測試結果較快且穩定，我們險勝。

1. **run neck-and-neck** 不相上下

The two teams in the finale are running neck-and-neck.

總決賽的這兩組不相上下。

2. **fill me in** 告訴我情況

A: Do you know what's happened yesterday in the office.

B: No. Please fill me in.

A: 你知道昨天辦公室發生什麼事嗎？

B: 我不知道耶，告訴我。

  句型解析

"win by a nose" 源自於賽馬競賽中，第一名僅以馬鼻子般距離險勝第二名，表示戰況激烈僅以些微差距險勝。

另外，**"win by a length"** 這裡的 length 代表馬匹一個身體的長度，表示以明顯差距勝利。而 **"win by a neck"** 則是介於上述兩者之間的差距。

"neck-and-neck" (adj. adv.) 看到兩匹馬一會前一會後，不相上下，表示兩方戰況激烈不分勝負。

"win in a photo finish" 表示難分勝負，結果必須用影像分析，才能判定。

句型延伸及範例

1. The quarterly shipment report is out. Our competitor won by a nose in the smartphone sector.

   這季度的出貨報告出來了，競爭對手在智慧手機領域些微領先。

2. Our company won by a length in the high-end lens production category. Congratulations to the entire design team.

   本公司高端鏡頭產品生產類別裡明顯領先其他同業。恭喜所有設計團隊的人員。

WEEK 10

Win by a Nose

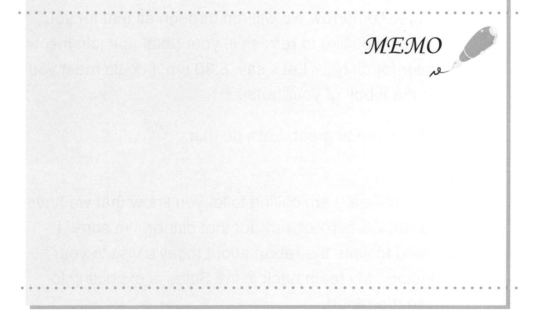

MEMO

Take a Rain Check

改期

 **Dialogue**

After the factory tour

科技業無往不利的英語力

Melissa: Peggy, what do you think about our factory?

Peggy: It looks great. The people seem professional and the facility is modern. I would still like to see the warehouse management and inventory control mechanism.

Melissa: Sure. Tomorrow we will run through all that for you. Would you like to refresh in your hotel and join me later for dinner? Let's say, 6.30 pm. I could meet you in the lobby of your hotel.

Peggy: That sounds great. Let's do that.

(A while later)

Peggy: Hi, Melissa. I am calling to let you know that we have to **take a rain check** for that dinner. I'm sorry. I need to write the report about today's visit to your factory. My team back in the Sates is expecting to see the report.

Melissa: No problem. We'll play it by ear.

 對話譯文

工廠參觀後

Melissa : **Peggy**，妳對我們的工廠看法如何？

Peggy : 看起來很不錯。員工都很專業和設施很先進。不過，我想看看倉儲管理與庫存管控的機制。

Melissa : 當然。明天我們會展示倉庫系統運作方式和庫存管理系統。妳想先回飯店梳洗一下，晚點一起吃飯？比如說傍晚 6 點半，我到妳的飯店的大廳等妳。

Peggy : 好啊，就這麼說定。

（過了一會兒……）

Peggy : 嗨，**Melissa**，我打電話來告訴妳，吃飯可能要改天了。很抱歉我需要將今天的工廠視察報告準備完畢，我在美國的團隊希望看到這報告。

Melissa : 沒問題，讓我們看情況再說。

科技關鍵知識用語

1. mechanism Ⓝ 機制

The whole waste process mechanism is run by solar energy.

這整個廢棄物處理機制是用太陽能運作的。

2. the States (=United States of America) 美國

你會常聽到美國人會用 the States 來代表美國

My wife is back in the States.

我太太回去美國。

3. play it by ear (= improvise) 隨興所至，視情況而定，到時候再說

A: What is you plan tomorrow? Would you like to go fishing?

B: I have no plan and let's play it by ear.

A：你明天有什麼計畫？想去釣魚嗎？

B：我沒有什麼計畫，讓我們到時候再說。

 句型解析

"take a rain check" 源自球賽術語，因下雨球賽需延後，但你所買的觀賽球票仍有效，待球賽繼續，仍可持票入場。因此在工作場合中，因約好的活動必須改期則可告訴對方 "Let's take a rain check." 「讓我們改期」，這種說法並非取消而是改期，也清楚表明很希望能參與，但不幸須改期。"postpone"「延期」有類似的用法，但 "take a rain check" 是更口語化的說法。

句型延伸及範例

1. I am not feeling well. I might have to take a rain check for that drink.

   我有點不舒服,我可能要改天才能跟你喝兩杯了。

2. Let's postpone the dinner appointment to another day.

   讓我們將晚餐的約會延至另一天。

3. Could we have the dinner another day?

   我們能不能改天吃飯好嗎?

   (這種說法有時會給人你並不是很想跟對方吃飯的猜想。)

Field the Question/ Field That

 **Dialogue**

科技業無往不利的英語力

Customer: Thank you for your presentation. It has been an informative and inspiring session. We got some great ideas about ways we may benefit from your expertise. We believe this would be a win-win situation. Before we close our meeting today, I have one last question: how exactly would we move ahead together from here?

Project leader: Amy is the account manager. Amy, would you like to **field that**?

Amy: Sure. First of all, a memo of understanding and a confidentiality agreement would be drawn up for both parties to sign. This would be followed by the exchange of project and technical information. From there we can sit down and discuss ways to proceed further.

 對話譯文

客戶：謝謝你們今天的簡報，提供相當多的資訊和令人興奮的內容。我們已有些想法如何借助貴公司的專業來合作，相信這是一個雙贏局面。在結束今天的會議前，最後只有一個問題：我們該如何進行？

專案負責人：Amy 是客戶經理。Amy，你願意回答這問題嗎？

Amy：當然。首先，會準備備忘錄和保密合約讓雙方會簽，然後就可以交換技術內容和需求。之後我們就能夠坐下來談談如何進行下一步。

 科技關鍵知識用語

1.expertise ⓝ 專業技術

We have recognized your expertise. Unfortunately, that is not what the position requires.

我們知道你具有相當的專業，只可惜並不是這工作所需的領域。

2. **win-win** 雙贏

This is a win-win proposal.

這是個雙贏的提案。

3. **move ahead** 進行下一步(= move on = proceed further)

I think we can stop the discussion and move ahead now.

我認為我們可以不要再討論進行下一步了。

4. **memo (memorandum) of understanding = MOU** 備忘錄

5. **followed by** 接著，跟著

She is followed by a group of little kids.

她的後面跟著一群小孩子。

💡 句型解析

"field the question" 或是 "field that" 源自棒球的專用術語，當有外野區的高飛球，球員會依距離和位置情況選擇是否前去接外野球，同時喊出 "I can field that one"「我來接」。而用於商業對話則是某人去回答特定的問題；尤其在一個會議討論中，可能主管會決定誰是適合回這問題的人，亦或是某人覺得他願意回答這一問題，則可主動提出 "I will field that"「我來回答」。

科技業無往不利的英語力

1. Tom, I can field that question.
   Tom，我可以回答這個問題。

2. Leslie, would you mind fielding that?
   Leslie，你介意回答這問題嗎？

Deep/Shallow Bench

人才很多/不足

Dialogue

Alex: Hi, Ellen. May I speak to you for a minute about allocation of our resources?

Ellen: Sure. I have been wanting to talk to you about this. After losing two very talented senior R&D engineers, we're left with a **shallow bench**.
For the project we are trying to launch, our competitor is now positioned in our red zone. If we can't submit a credible proposal soon they will get the touchdown.

Alex: I recognize that, too. We face a challenge allocating our engineers now among all the projects we have on our hands. Our new recruits aren't helping much.
We need to consider hiring more experienced people, investing in more training for new employees, or outsourcing some tasks.

科技業無往不利的英語力

 對話譯文

Alex：嗨，Ellen。我可以跟你談談我們的資源分配問題嗎？

Ellen：當然，我也正想和你談談這件事。兩個我們非常有能力的資深R&D工程師離開之後，我們能出場打戰的人不多。
對於我們正要執行的案子，競爭對手現在處於有利位置，若我們再不提出企畫書給客戶，他們就拿到案子了。

Alex：我知道這一點。對我們手上的案子，我們的工程師分配有很大的問題，而新加入的沒法幫太多的忙。
我們必須考慮找更多有經驗的人，或對新進員工投資更多的訓練，不然就是外包一些工作。

科技關鍵知識用語

1.allocation ⓝ 分配

We don't get enough rainfall in last few months. Our water supply is going to be on allocation.

在過去數個月沒有得到足夠的降雨,我們將進行限水。

2.in the red zone (American football)(= in a strong position to move ahead) 處於有利位置

We are in the red zone to score.

我們在得分的有利位置。

~源自美式足球,球員在進行下一波攻勢的紅色區域,表示位於有利攻擊位置

3.touchdown 達陣得分,成功

When the hometown team scored a touchdown, the crowd yelled and cheered.

當地主隊達陣得分的時候,群眾都歡呼了起來。

4.outsource ⓥ 外包

Due to the manpower shortage. It has left us with no choice to outsource the projects.

由於人手短缺,讓我們沒有選擇必須外包案子。

句型解析

"deep/shallow bench" 源自於球賽用語，在球場上的長椅子上可以備戰的球員隊伍陣容，主要是後援的優秀球員。"deep bench"表示能上場比賽的後援優秀人手很多。

"shallow bench" 表示能上場應戰的人數有限，造成熱門球員無法休息。

當用於商場上時，"deep/shallow bench" 表示你的團隊中能獨立作戰優秀員工的陣容。

句型延伸及範例

1. Charlotte and Brad speak well in public. After them we have a shallow bench. Let the two of them carry most of the presentation.
   Charlotte 和 Brad 在公開場合能侃侃而談。除了他們，我們團隊中找不到其他人能做簡報，所以將大部分的報告都交給他們兩位來擔任。

2. Thanks to our recent recruitment of some very experienced engineers, we have a deep bench.
   隨著近期招聘的業內非常有經驗的人才，我們的強打人手不少。

Playbook

 **Dialogue**

A: It is no longer a far-fetched notion that Apple could be developing an electric connected car. If so, this could change the market landscape for auto-driving cars.

I am eager to know what Apple's competitors have in their **playbook** to help them keep up.

A product of that sort would definitely give competitors a run for their money.

B: That is the beauty of the high-tech industry. Now and then you see a revolutionary development inspire everyone to greater creativity.

科技業無往不利的英語力

 對話譯文

A： 蘋果正在開發一款電動無線連接汽車，而這不再是一個難以置信的想法。真是如此，蘋果將改變自動駕駛車市場的整個格局。

我很熱切想知道其他競爭對手的應對戰略中要如何去跟進。

這類型的產品肯定會與其他競爭對手進行激烈競爭。

B： 這就是在高科技產業工作美妙的部分，三不五時，你就會看到革命性的創新和聽到令人鼓舞的想法。

科技關鍵知識用語

1. **far-fetched** 難以置信
Very soon, a trip to Mars won't be a far-fetched idea.
很快的，到火星旅行將不再會是令人難以置信的想法了。

2. **keep up** 跟上速度（腳步）
Please keep up with the group. Don't drop behind.
請跟上大家的腳步，不要落後。

3. give someone a run for one's money

不讓……輕易取勝，與……進行激烈競爭

We plan to give him a run for his money.

我們計劃不讓他輕易取勝。

4. now and then　偶而，有時候 (=from time to time)

Now and then, she disappears for a few days.

她偶而會消失幾天。

 句型解析

"playbook" 中文有如「教戰手冊」或「孫子兵法」。原本意思是一本舞台劇本，但在運動球賽上（尤其是美式足球）比喻為「戰略」，尤其教練有一套套的應戰策略，"playbook" 中的一頁頁可以是教練的一個個球賽包括上場球員和戰略打法。用於商場上，則比喻為一個產品或行銷策略的整套計畫書。

句型延伸及範例

1. Samsung has adopted a design strategy like this before. That solution was right out of their Galaxy Note playbook.

   三星之前已經有採用過類似這樣的設計策略，這完全是由他們的 Galaxy Note策略而來。

2. The CEO thinks we can sell mobile devices the same way we once sold computers. It holds us back. New technologies require new marketing playbooks.

   執行長認為我們可以用之前販售電腦的策略來賣手機。這讓我們猶豫不決。新的科技需要新的完整行銷策略計畫。

MEMO

Slam Dunk

勝券在握

 Dialogue

Sylvia: Hi, John. I have some good news for you from Barcelona.

I met the UAE's largest retailer at our Barcelona conference last week. They really like our new virtual reality headset. Give them a call today about a contract.

It looks like a **slam dunk**. Here is the company's contact information and a copy of the minutes from our meeting. Good luck!

John: Indeed, this is great news. Thanks for the sales lead!

 對話譯文

Sylvia：嗨，**John**。我從巴塞隆那給你帶來了一個好消息。

我在上週在巴塞隆那舉行的產品發表會遇到中東最大零售商。這家公司對我們新推出可以親身體驗虛擬實境的耳機感到非常興奮，今天就打電話給他們談合約吧。

我相信這筆訂單勝券在握。這是合約資料和與他們談的會議記要。祝你好運！

John：確實是，這是個大好消息。感謝你的這一個業務信息。

科技關鍵知識用語

1. minutes from the meeting (= meeting minutes) 會議記錄

As per the meeting minutes, we are supposed to send a contract to them today.

根據會議記錄，我們今天應把合約送給他們。

2. sales lead 業務信息

It is your priority to collect all the sales leads during the exhibition.

在展覽中，你的首要任務就是收集業務信息。

科技業無往不利的英語力

 句型解析

"slam dunk"中文翻譯為「灌籃」，不用多解釋，大家都應該知道這是籃球中的灌籃動作。因此用在商業中解釋為「勝券在握」，「輕而易舉」。

1. That customer is eager to sign a deal for our updated product. Give her a call. It's a slam dunk.

   那個客戶非常急迫地想要簽下我們最新的產品。打電話給她,訂單已到手。

2. The election was a slam dunk for our side. We got more than 70% of the vote.

   選舉證明我們的絕對勝利,我們得了70%以上的票數。

3. The evidence against the defendant is overwhelming. For the prosecutor this case is a slam dunk.

   這個不利於被告的證據具有壓倒性的關鍵。對於檢方而言,這個案件的勝利在握。

4. Give the calendar app project to Sally. She can phone it in because she has programmed space satellites before.

   把這一個日曆應用程式案子交給Sally。她曾寫過人造衛星的程式,對她而言這是小意思。

   (I can phone it in. = It is easy for me. 另一種表示輕而易舉的說法,表示本身技能超過所需技能)

Next Play

下一個戰略

 **Dialogue**

General Manager: Our competitor launched its new flagship device last week with an aggressive ad campaign and PR push. It got glowing reviews and now the sales are leaving us in the dust. What's our **next play**?

Business Director: To be honest, they caught us off guard. After three years of declining sales this is a huge comeback for them. We are organizing a meeting of all our functional leaders. We need to sit down and evaluate the new situation.

General Manager: Keep me posted about the results of your group discussion. We're losing ground. We need to make a play soon.

296

對話譯文

總經理： 我們的競爭對手上週推出了他們的旗艦產品，加上積極的廣告宣傳和公關的強力推宣傳，獲得非常好評的報導，我們的銷售現在望塵莫及。我們的下一個戰略是什麼？

業務總監： 說實話，他們是出奇不意，已低迷了三年，這對他們來說是個大的反轉。我安排了個會議，要所有各部門的主管來全盤討論。

總經理： 隨時讓我知道討論之後的情況，我們需要盡快決定下一步棋。

 科技關鍵知識用語

1.flagship　ⓝ　旗艦，主打

It is my honor to present you our flagship product of the year.

是我的榮幸向您介紹我們主打年度最佳產品。

2.glowing reviews　大獲好評報導(= highly positive reviews)

We got glowing review for the new device.

我們的新產品獲非常好的報導。

3. **leave someone in the dust**　望塵莫及

Her fluent English speaking has left us in the dust.

他一口流利的英文讓我們都望塵莫及。

When she went to study in USA, she couldn't speak a word of English. Ten years later her English leaves us in the dust.

當她去美國唸書時，她一句英文也不會說。**10**年之後，她的英文讓我們每個人都望塵莫及。

4. **off guard**　鬆懈(= unprepared; not watching)

One of the budget airlines caught the competition off guard yesterday by announcing a big drop in fares.

其中一個廉價航空昨天出其不備宣布票價大降價。

5. **comeback**　回復，東山再起

They decided to have a big drop on the price for a comeback in market share.

他們決定大降價來重返市場佔有率。

 句型解析

"**next play**" 在職場中，通常指得是「下一個戰略」，前面的單元中有提到 "**playbook**" 是美式足球中適用的專業術語，"**play**" 本是舞台劇中的劇本之說，但用於美式足球中，則代表球賽中的戰略，包括進攻和防守的各式戰略和位置部署，進而將其用於商業術語，"**play**" 也代表策略計畫。"**make the play**"「策定戰略」，"**run the play**"「執行戰略計畫」，

"our next play"「下一部戰略」。
playmaker「策定戰略者」

 句型延伸及範例

1.We have finished this quarter poorly. The revenue is much behind the target. What's our next play?
我們這個季度表現不佳，收入數字離目標很遠。我們的下一步棋是什麼？

2.We lost the top spot in market share. What play can we call to recover it?
我已經失去市場占有率的第一名位置。有什麼策略再站回第一名呢？

3.Charlene is our playmaker for public presentations. During the Q&A let her carry the ball.
Charlene 是我們團隊準備公開簡報時的決策者。Q&A 的時候，讓她上場。

Leader 017

科技業無往不利的英語力

作　　者　Teresa Chou
封面構成　高鍾琪
內頁構成　菩薩蠻數位文化有限公司

發 行 人　周瑞德
企劃編輯　陳欣慧
校　　對　陳韋佑、饒美君
印　　製　大亞彩色印刷製版股份有限公司
初　　版　2015 年 4 月
定　　價　新台幣 349 元
出　　版　力得文化
電　　話　(02) 2351-2007
傳　　真　(02) 2351-0887
地　　址　100　台北市中正區福州街 1 號 10 樓之 2
E - m a i l　best.books.service@gmail.com

港澳地區總經銷　泛華發行代理有限公司
地　　　　址　香港新界將軍澳工業邨駿昌街 7 號 2 樓
電　　　　話　(852) 2798-2323
傳　　　　真　(852) 2796-5471

國家圖書館出版品預行編目(CIP)資料

科技業無往不利的英語力 / Teresa Chou 著. --
初版. -- 臺北市 : 力得文化, 2015.04
　面 ;　公分. -- (Leader ; 17)
ISBN 978-986-91458-6-2(平裝)

1.英文 2.科技業 3.句法

805.169　　　　　　　　　104005331

力得文化
Leader Culture

Lead your way. Be your own leader!

力得文化
Leader Culture

Lead your way. Be your own leader!